Jean's Discovery

The Uncovered Gene: Book One

K. Redd

First edition

Print ISBN: 979-8-9861449-4-8

E-Book ISBN: 979-8-9861449-3-1

Library of Congress Control Number: 2024900585

Cover art by MiblArt

Editing by Tory Hunter

Editing by Beth Rodgers

"Sometimes when you lose your way, you find YOURSELF."

—— Mandy Hale

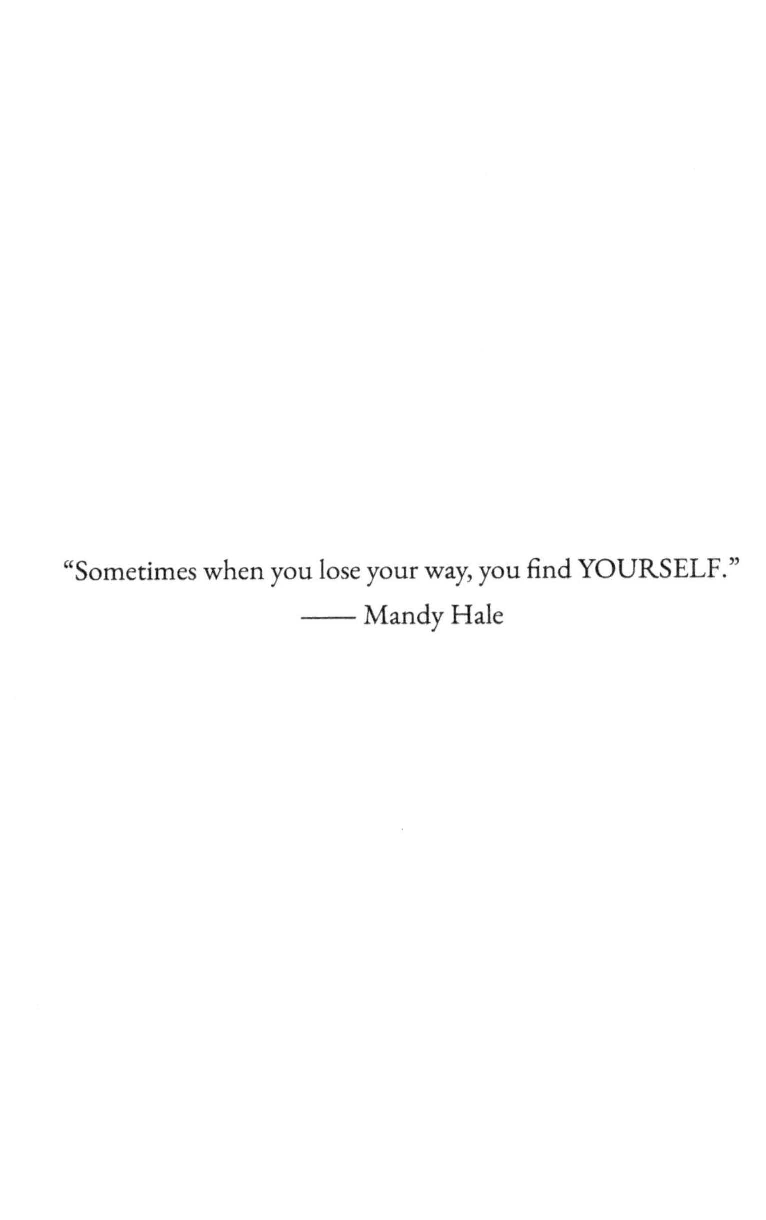

Contents

PROLOGUE

Thunder boomed as random sparks of lightning flitted across the midnight sky. Rain pelted Mary's windshield in heavy sheets. Tears blurred her vision as she drove down the winding, wooded road near a local farm. She was late and her phone reception had died. This was not the time or place to get lost. As Mary pulled into the meeting spot, a few feet away from another car, the other vehicle's headlights flashed, and a woman exited it carrying an enormous umbrella. Mary rolled down her window and dabbed the corners of her eye with a tissue. The tears surprised her because she was normally so strong-willed.

"I was scared you weren't gonna make it," the woman said as rain gushed off her umbrella like a waterfall.

"Yeah, I almost turned around several times."

The woman peeked into the back window. "Don't you worry. We'll take good care of her. I have a very close friend who is a social worker in the Department of Family Services. We'll keep you updated."

Mary sighed. "I know. I just wish it didn't have to be this way." She stepped out of her vehicle and walked to the back door as the woman held the umbrella over her. She lifted her newborn's car seat out and followed the woman to her car. After fastening the baby into the back seat, Mary leaned down and gently kissed her forehead. "I love you." More tears flowed from the corners of Mary's eyes. She tucked a small note into the car seat with pertinent information, such as the baby's date of birth and first name. The note also contained a few sentences stating that she couldn't keep the baby, but hoped Jean would be placed with a loving family.

The woman escorted Mary back to her car. "I'll call you tomorrow," she said before sprinting back to her vehicle.

Mary watched as the woman started the engine and disappeared into the distance. She had never felt so heartbroken, giving away the baby she loved so much after spending less than twenty-four hours with her.

Mary headed back home, her heart heavy with sorrow. She couldn't stop thinking about the little bundle of joy she had just given away. The baby's tiny fingers and toes, the button nose, the perfect soft coos that melted her heart. But as much as it hurt, Mary knew she had made the right decision. Her daughter's life depended on it.

When Mary arrived home, there were two unfamiliar, large black Hummers parked in front of her house. As she pulled closer, two men wearing black raincoats walked toward her front door. She broke into a sweat as her heartbeat thrummed in her ears, so she backed up and sped away.

Glancing in the rearview mirror every few minutes, she drove for hours while her thoughts were a jumbled mess. *Why were those men at my house? Are they coming to take my baby or am I just being paranoid? What if Caroline was wrong? Was she a delusional nutcase with a vendetta against Gravin?*

As she drove down the empty street toward the highway, Mary's mind wandered back to the baby she had just given away. *Is she safe? Will I ever see her again? Will they make sure she's placed with a loving foster family? Will she be angry at me for giving her up? And what about abandonment issues? Will she suffer from mental health issues? I guess I'll have no choice but to accept her decision if she never wants to meet...*

A shrill tone pierced the silence, and Mary glanced at her cellphone. Her heart raced when the words "Private Number" flashed on the screen. With her hands trembling, she pressed the talk button on the center console to answer. "Hello?"

"Is this Mary Calloway?" a man asked.

Mary's chest tightened. Who was this? How did he get her number? *I should hang up. No, what if it's Caroline's associate? I can always hang up if it's nothing.* "Yes, who is this?" she managed, hoping her fear wasn't obvious.

"This is Dr. Gravin, from Genesis Fertility. You missed your appointment today."

Mary's knuckles whitened as she gripped the steering wheel tighter. Swallowing hard, she racked her brain for a plausible excuse.

"Is everything okay?" Dr. Gravin pressed when Mary failed to respond. "We can reschedule you for tomorrow. Does that work for you?"

Mary blinked, hot tears escaping down her cheeks. She had no choice but to lie. "I'm sorry, Doctor. I can't talk now." She paused, taking a shaky breath. "I lost the baby."

Dr. Gravin was silent for a moment. "Oh, I'm sorry to hear that," he said, skepticism creeping into his voice. "When ... when did it happen?"

"Last night." Mary hastily grabbed a tissue out of her purse. "My midwife handled everything. I can't talk now. Bye." She ended the call with trembling fingers and flung the phone out the window. Gripping the wheel, Mary drove aimlessly down I-90, before exiting the highway. Dr. Gravin's suspicious words echoed through her mind. She was sure he didn't believe her.

Mary headed down a dark, deserted road. It had been hours since she recognized her surroundings. Her knuckles ached from the intense grip on the steering wheel. Her breath came in gasps as the suspicion in Dr. Gravin's words echoed in her mind. He knew. Somehow, he knew she had lied about losing the baby.

Panic constricted Mary's chest. *What do they want with my daughter? To sell her to the highest bidder? For experiments? Or something far more sinister?* She blinked away fresh tears, trying to clear the blurriness from her vision. Up ahead, the highway loomed, offering a route distancing her from the terror at home.

Mary knew she had to disappear completely, to protect herself and the perfect, innocent life she had just brought into this world. As she veered onto the highway ramp, she whispered a prayer for her daughter's safety. She had no clue where she would end up. But she knew she would do whatever it took to make sure her baby had a chance at a better future. Gripping the wheel tighter, she drove onward into the dark unknown.

1

New Beginnings

As the sunset's crimson and yellow fingers hugged the horizon, Jean's father clasped her hand and gently squeezed it, the familiar callouses and warmth steadying her trembling fingers. Jean blinked back tears stinging her eyes as her father handed her a battered silver suitcase—the final severing of her childhood moorings.

"Do you need help with anything before we leave?" Mr. Anderson asked flatly, his face betraying his emotion.

Jean flashed a slight wisp of a smile. "No, I'm all set."

Mrs. Anderson's eyes filled with tears as she wrapped her arms around Jean in a crushing embrace. "I can't believe how time flew. If you ever need anything, just call. Remember, you can always switch to the community college. It's so much closer." She pulled back, hands lingering on Jean's shoulders.

"Mom, don't worry. Everything will be alright. I'll visit so much you'll get sick of me," Jean said in a reassuring tone.

Mrs. Anderson tenderly kissed Jean's forehead, the touch sending a comforting shiver down her spine. "Yeah, well, I worry so much," her mother replied, her voice filled with both pride and concern. "You'll always be my little girl. Promise me you'll take your vitamins every day, study hard, and eat right."

Jean's heart swelled with love as she locked eyes with her mother's. "I promise."

"Okay, we'll see you on Thanksgiving, but let me know if you want to come for a visit sooner."

Nervous energy filled Jean's entire body as she lugged her last suitcase down the hallway and into her dorm room. She sighed heavily as she opened the door to the small, bland space featuring three loft beds and matching desks lined up against different walls. A pang of uncertainty pierced Jean's stomach as she surveyed the room and thought about her first day of high school four years ago.

As she entered Mountain Ridge High to begin her freshman year, optimism filled Jean's heart. New school, new teachers, and hundreds of other students to meet awaited her. She grinned as she glanced at her class schedule. *English, Ms. Green, room 103.* Dodging crowds of students walking in every direction, Jean scurried down the hallway and entered Ms. Green's room. *Great, I don't see any of the bullies.* She sat at a desk next to a petite, brunette girl who greeted her with a warm, inviting smile. Before long, more students began filing into the room.

"Oh look, it's Ms. Freak," Petra shrieked as she entered the classroom.

Jean blinked her eyes and returned her thoughts to the present. Her eyes surveyed the dorm room. *It's time to stop dwelling on the past and start living life in the present. I doubt I'll ever see those bullies again.* Jean let go of her suitcase's handle as she took a deep inhale of the dust-filled air and her mouth curled into a grin.

The following morning, Jean headed to her campus tour. As she crossed the quad, the hair on the back of her neck prickled. She paused and glanced over her shoulder. A lady standing next to a tree stared at her. Shaking off the uneasy feeling, she hugged her arms around herself and continued walking. When she arrived at the tour meeting spot in the Student Union, she scribbled on a nametag and stood near her assigned guide in a group of fifty students. She suddenly had a feeling of déjà vu as she watched everyone else engaging in introductions and small talk. *I should just walk up to someone and introduce myself.* Spotting a student standing by herself, Jean strolled toward her. Just as she was about to say "hi," another student greeted the target and hugged her. *Oh, they must be friends from high school.* Jean sighed. *I guess I'll stay by myself. It would be rude to interrupt them.*

By the end of the tour, most of the other students acted like new best friends after gathering in small groups. In contrast, Jean received polite smiles and diverted glances when she made eye contact with others. She couldn't wait to meet her roommates. Surely, they would become close friends, living in a small, confined area.

After the campus tour, Jean entered a large auditorium for the session on class registration when a man's eyes bore into her. As soon as her eyes met with the man's eyes, he turned and walked away. She shivered. Was it her imagination? The long day filled with campus tours and orientation sessions was exhausting, so she was happy when she could finally return to her dorm room.

"Hey, are you going to the welcome barbecue tonight?" a cheerful voice called out from across the hallway as Jean unlocked her door. She looked up to see a girl with short, spiky, black hair and a circular barbell nose ring leaning against the corridor wall.

"Um, yeah, I was thinking about it," Jean stammered, trying to sound comfortable despite the pounding in her chest. Jean took a couple of deep breaths to relax her mind and body.

The girl smiled. "Great! Perhaps I'll see you there. By the way, I'm Laci," the girl said as she extended her hand.

"I'm Jean," Jean replied as she shook Laci's hand. As Laci disappeared back into her own room, Jean turned toward her room. A young lady stood next to her door talking on a cellphone. *Is that one of my roommates?* When Jean continued walking toward her door, the young lady glanced at Jean and abruptly turned, heading to the nearby staircase.

Jean opened her door. Her roommates had moved in while she was at orientation. Clothes and duffel bags littered one bed, while the other was neatly made up with flowery bedding. Photographs lined the wall next to the neatly made-up bed. Jean perused the photos, wondering what her roommates were like. *Will they be friendly and nice? Or will they be like those bullies in school?* Thoughts of the torment she endured throughout her school years made Jean's pulse quicken. During high school, she gave up on developing friendships with her peers and mostly chatted with teachers and school personnel during school hours.

As Jean looked at the smiling faces in the photos, she relaxed. She wasn't sure which person in the photos was her roommate, but everyone looked nice. All the faces were filled with warm smiles instead of smug expressions. Her roommate also seemed to be adventurous, as there were pictures of people doing things like hiking and skydiving. Jean stooped down and leaned closer to the pictures. The same person appeared in most of them. *Hmm, the one with the auburn hair must be my roommate. It looks like she has blonde hair sometimes. Oh, it looks like she also sometimes has black hair.* Jean giggled. *She must be a cool person.*

That evening, as she walked to the barbecue, Jean reminded herself that all freshmen were the same — new students trying to make friends and fit in with others. But as she approached the event, a light orange glow emanated from her fingertips. *Oh no, not again.* The last time Jean saw the strange glow was on her eighteenth birthday. She had assumed it was from a nearby streetlight, but she was in the middle of the quad surrounded by four tall dorms and there were no streetlights on. Jean quickly shoved her hands into her pockets, hoping no one else had seen it. Standing near the entrance to where the barbecue was located, she tried to decide what to do. Barbecue smoke wafted through the air, flooding her nostrils. *This was probably a bad idea. I should leave.* Jean turned around to return to her room when she heard a familiar voice.

"Hey, Jean! Over here!"

Jean glanced over her shoulder. Her neighbor Laci was enthusiastically waving her arms in the air.

"Hey, Laci, right?" Jean said, trying to sound more self-assured than she felt.

Laci looked up from her conversation with another girl and smiled at her. "That's right! I'm glad you made it," she said warmly. "This is Tessa. Tessa, this is my neighbor, Jean."

"Hey," Tessa said, waving.

Jean returned the gesture and grinned, feeling a flicker of hope that she could make friends in college. *Crap, I forgot about my glowing hands.* Jean lowered her eyes, peeking at her hands. *Great! The glow is gone.* As she walked closer to Laci and Tessa, Jean glanced at the table of food. "So, what's good?" Laci and Tessa exchanged glances and giggled.

"Actually, we were just talking about how terrible it is. We might have been better off going to the cafeteria," Tessa said.

"The burgers aren't horrible. They're a little dry and bland, but with ketchup, they aren't too bad," Laci said as she chomped into a hamburger.

Jean grabbed a paper plate and topped it with grilled chicken, potato salad, a hot dog, and baked beans. She walked to where Tessa and Laci were sitting and bit into a chicken wing. It was bland and difficult to chew. After scooping up some of the potato salad and sticking it into her mouth, Jean grimaced. "Yeah, this definitely makes me homesick for my mom's food."

Tessa and Laci giggled. "If cafeteria food tastes anything like this, we'll need to have regular pizza nights," Tessa said.

Jean glanced at her hands. They had a dull glow. *Not again!* She looked at Tessa and Laci. *Hopefully, they didn't notice anything.* She hopped up and set the plate of food on top of her palms. "I think I've had enough of this food. I'll see you guys later. I'm going to head back to my room to finish unpacking."

Tessa waved. "Don't forget pizza night. Let me know when you're interested."

When Jean arrived back at her room, a girl was unpacking a suitcase and shoving clothes into drawers.

"Howdy! Ya must be Jean!" the girl exclaimed with her voice in a slight southern drawl as she extended her hand for a friendly shake. "Oh my gosh, you are so pretty! I'm Emmie, your new roommate. Did ya meet our other roommate, Carmen?"

Jean grinned. It was the first time someone other than her parents called her pretty. "Thanks for the compliment. No, I haven't met her yet. Is she here?"

"Yeah, but she went out to eat with her family."

"Oh, okay," Jean replied, trying to hide her nervousness. Emmie had already decorated her side of the room with photos adorning the wall, a small, colorful rug in front of her desk, and a blue recycling bin. Jean set her plate on her desk and started unpacking her suitcase.

"Ya need help with anything?" Emmie asked. "I have some extra hangers if you need 'em."

"No, thank you. I don't need any." Jean glanced at her hands to see if the strange glow was still coming from them. Fortunately, it was gone. *The sun must have hit them a certain way. No one has hands that glow. Wait, there wasn't any sun.* Jean re-directed her attention to Emmie. "I like your pictures. You must be real adventurous."

Emmie tossed her wavy auburn hair to the side. "Yeah, I guess ya could say that. So, tell me about yourself, roomie. Do ya have any interesting hobbies? Have ya decided on a major? What are your life goals?"

Jean chuckled. "Well, I don't have any interesting hobbies unless you consider watching cheesy romance movies to be a hobby. I haven't decided on a major, but I'm considering genealogy, history, or biology. Life goals. Let's see. I guess my number one life goal is to find my parents."

Emmie's eyes widened as she gasped. "You lost your parents?"

"Oh, no. I mean my birth parents. I'm adopted. I love my adoptive parents and they're great, but I would like to know who my biological parents are."

"Well, in that case, I hope ya find your parents. Have you ever thought about doing one of those DNA tests to find them? I signed up for a family history class that has a DNA test as a class assignment."

"I signed up for that class, too. We can study together."

A lock clicked, and the door swung open. A young woman with flowing blonde hair sauntered into the room with two middle-aged adults and a young girl. "Hi," she muttered.

"Howdy, Carmen and family. This is our roommate, Jean. We were just getting to know each other," Emmie exclaimed with a wide grin.

Carmen gave a curt nod toward Jean and directed her attention to her family. She muttered something to her parents and gave them a brusque hug.

Carmen's mother kissed her on the forehead. "I'll call to check up on you later tonight."

"Well, you better hurry if you want to beat traffic," Carmen said, glancing at her watch as she opened the door for her family to leave. "Bye."

Jean's shoulders tensed as Carmen slammed the door. *Hopefully, she's just tired. She doesn't seem nearly as friendly as Emmie.* Jean chuckled to herself. *This will be interesting. They seem like polar opposites. Emmie has more of a grunge vibe while Carmen is a high fashion princess. And me, I am … well, I don't know what I am. I guess I'm somewhere in the middle. I wonder which part of the roommate questionnaire caused them to put us together.*

After her parents left, Carmen grabbed her chair and dragged it near Jean and Emmie. "So, what did I miss?" She slid a small mirror out of her pocket and held in front of her face, smoothing her hair.

"Well," Emmie said with excitement in her voice, "she's adopted, and guess what? We just found out that we're both enrolled in the same family history class."

"Cool," Carmen replied, slipping the mirror back into her pocket. "Is family history supposed to be interesting? I still have to choose two more classes."

Emmie's voice filled with delight as she squealed, "Ooh, you should definitely join us! We can study together, and trust me, it'll be an easy A."

After a brief pause, Carmen shrugged. "Maybe I will," she said, her voice tinged with a hint of uncertainty.

"So, are you guys gonna join any clubs or pledge a sorority?" Emmie asked.

"I'm pledging my mom's sorority," Carmen said, tossing and fluffing her hair.

Jean tilted her head. *Hmm, a club might be a good idea. It would be a great way to meet people.* "I haven't looked at the list. Are there any interesting clubs?"

Emmie's eyes lit up as she scrolled through the club descriptions on her laptop. "Ya name it, there's a club for it. Archery, dance, drama, figure skating. Ya'll, there's even a UFO watcher's club," she said, chuckling. "Ooh, there's an environmental club, too. I'm definitely gonna join that." Emmie hopped up and headed to her closet. "Speaking of which, I've noticed far too many plastic bags coming into this room." She emerged with two cotton canvas bags and handed one to Jean and Carmen. "My gift to you. Take it whenever you go shopping, so you won't need to use a plastic bag."

"Thanks. Isn't there something in a couple of days where the clubs set up tables with information? I'll probably stop by there to see if anything interests me," Jean said.

"Cool, I'll go with you. Wanna join us, Carmen?"

"Sure, I'm down for checking it out," Carmen said, pulling a hand mirror out of her purse. "So, where is everyone from? I'll start. I'm from Los Angeles."

"That's a good question. My parents were military, so I spent a lot of time in different countries. I lived in various states as well. Texas, Virginia, Alabama. We spent the last two years in Montana, so I guess that's where I'm from now," Emmie said.

Jean hesitated, her eyes downcast, and her shoulders slumped. "I lived in Montana my entire life," she muttered, rubbing her arm as she leaned back in her chair.

"Cool. I love, love, love Montana. Off topic, but I just noticed something. Jean, what color are your eyes?" Emmie asked.

"Brown, why?"

"Oh, I didn't mean anything by it. They're beautiful, but your pupils suddenly started looking closer to yellow. I don't know. It might be the lighting," Emmie said.

Jean shuddered and scrunched her face up in worry. There seemed to be something strange happening to her eyes in the past, but she could never figure out what it was. She often thought she was imagining things or that the lighting affected her eye color. "I think my eyes might look a little different in different lightings," she said as she bounced her leg up and down. *I'm not sure what's up with my eyes. People keep mentioning my eyes changing colors. Perhaps it's time to invest in some color contact lenses. At least then my eyes will stay one color. But what will I do about the glow in my hands? I can't wear gloves every day.* She hopped up. "Hey, guys, I'm going to run to the bathroom."

As Jean cautiously walked down the dimly lit hallway, a sudden surge of fiery tingles erupted on her delicate skin, sending shivers down her spine. Panic gripped her, desperately pleading for this not to happen now, not in this moment. Yet, an otherworldly glow emanated from her trembling hands, gradually creeping up her arms like ethereal vines. Just a few steps away from reaching the sanctuary of the bathroom, her vision faltered, blurring the world around her. The floor seemed to lunge toward her, ruthlessly pulling her down as her body collapsed, trembling uncontrollably.

Amidst the chaos, a cacophony of voices swirled around Jean. "Someone call an ambulance!" one voice cried out, its tone laced with alarm. "What's on her arms?" another voice questioned, the curiosity tinged with fear. "Is she breathing?" echoed a voice laden with worry. Faces etched with distress encircled her fragile form. Dark tendrils of unconsciousness enveloped Jean, dragging her deeper into its enigmatic realm.

Jean peeled open her heavy lids, her eyes met by the piercing gaze of emergency medical technicians. The sterile scent of antiseptic filled her nostrils, mingling with the scent of fear hanging in the air. "I'm sorry," she uttered, her voice filled with a mix of vulnerability and determination, as she gingerly sat up. Taking a deep inhale, she tried to calm her racing heart. "I'm fine," she reassured everyone, her words carrying a hint of defiance.

One of the EMTs offered, "We can transport you to the hospital."

"No, that's okay. I'm fine."

A flicker of doubt passed through his eyes, the uncertainty clear in his tone. "Are you sure?"

With a nod and a faint smile, Jean replied, her voice steady, "Yeah." As she strolled back to her room, her mind spun, trying to make sense of what had just happened. Moments ago, a fiery rash had erupted down her arms, its eerie glow preceding a wave of weakness that felled her. Now, her skin was perfectly smooth, the episode almost like a faded nightmare.

Her thoughts drifted back to her high school biology class. A lecture on axolotl salamanders stuck in her mind. Her teacher had described their extraordinary ability to regenerate damaged tissue at a phenomenal rate, unlike any other animal. She had leaned forward, enraptured by accounts of the amphibians regrowing severed limbs with an embryonic-like power, unleashing mysterious cellular factors to heal without scarring within weeks.

Jean couldn't ignore the parallel or the reality she may harbor her own internal reservoir, allowing tissue regrowth and self-repair beyond normal human constraints. Perhaps a quirk of genetics or long-buried evolutionary legacy had flipped that switch for her. More questions than answers remained. But she was determined to unravel the biological secrets behind this strange gift and whether its origins held deeper truths about her yet-unknown lineage. It was no longer about wanting to discover information about her biological family. It was now about needing to find it.

2

Exploring New Territory

A heaviness settled in Jean's gut as her third-grade school group ascended the museum stairs. Head down, clutching her permission slip, she lagged behind her exuberant classmates. After a few steps, her squinted eyes drifted up to the clouds, losing herself in endless daydreams about traveling to other worlds.

"Jean! Pay attention," Ms. Wilkenson scolded.

Jean slid her group assignment card from her pocket and sighed. Of course, she got stuck with her least favorite people. The first was Petra, the class know-it-all who loved making fun of her. Petra was also the tallest and most athletic girl in the class, which was probably why she felt as if she could boss everyone around. The second enemy in-charge was Petra's best friend, Amber. Although not as tall, Amber always followed Petra's lead. She dressed like a fashion icon and often walked with a rhythmic stride, as if she was a model on a fashion show runway.

As the museum doors slid open, a chill slithered down Jean's spine. She lingered outside, wary of the strange symbols marking the entrance while her classmates charged ahead.

"Ew, Jean's going to infect the exhibits with her weirdness," Petra sneered, knocking into Jean's shoulder as she walked by. Jean winced. The other kids erupted in laughter. Heat flushed Jean's cheeks. She tried to ignore their teasing, but their words pierced like darts.

"Okay, quiet everyone." Ms. Wilkenson glanced up from a clipboard, grabbed the whistle dangling from the cord around her neck, took a deep breath and blew into the whistle. Ms. Wilkenson was a stout woman who barely stood taller than most of her students. "Quiet, everyone. Make sure you're with your assigned chaperone group."

Petra faced Jean and stuck out her tongue before raising her hand and skipping toward Ms. Wilkenson. "Mrs. W, Jean is in the wrong group."

Ms. Wilkenson wagged her finger. "Stop your nonsense. She's in the right group. Remember, if you become separated from the class, find the nearest museum employee. They will know how to locate us."

Petra wildly waved her arm. "Mrs. W.! Mrs. W.! Jean's eyes are glowing."

Ms. Wilkenson sighed as she peeked over the edge of her wire-frame glasses with her beady eyes. "What? Her eyes are growing?"

"Glowing. Her eyes are glowing. They look like a spooky monster," Petra said, leering at Jean as her mouth twisted into a smirk.

The entire class erupted in laughter, and Jean could feel her skin crawl as all eyes were on her. "Freak!" someone yelled.

Jean turned away from Petra and sighed. *Now, she's making up stuff about my eyes. What's next? I'm so sick of her. The sun is in my eyes. Doesn't she know what sunlight is?*

Ms. Wilkenson rolled her eyes and blew her whistle. "Quiet down, everyone. Now, I have one more thing to mention before we get started. Anyone who does not stay with their group and follow the chaperone's instructions will not participate in the class pizza party." Ms. Wilkenson glanced over her shoulder as the museum tour guide approached the class. "Okay, it looks like they're ready for us."

As Jean walked toward Ms. Bronson, Amber snuck up behind her, yanking her ponytail, pulling her curls taut. Petra and Amber giggled.

Ms. Bronson turned towards the girls and smiled. "What's so funny?"

"Oh nothing. Just a friend joke," Amber said.

"You don't want to share the friend joke with your mom?"

The tour guide displayed a wide, cheerful smile as she greeted them. "Welcome, everyone!" she sang in an overly perky voice. "The first exhibit is my absolute favorite in the entire museum. It's the space exhibit. The space exhibit will surround you with a digital galaxy as you explore the room. The exhibit also features human-like holograms, and a NASA-powered telescope along with rocks and other particles from outer space. Enjoy." The door slid open.

As soon as Jean entered, a rush of warmth filled her body. She paused in front of an illuminated display titled "Are We Alone?" Inside the glass case, a miniature UFO hovered above a model farm as a farmer stood, gaping in shock.

Jean imagined herself flying off into space, free from the bullies and the constant teasing. She wandered toward the end of the room, away from her chaperone group, and stared at the ceiling as stars glistened and planets rotated around the sun. Then she closed her eyes and imagined what it would be like to venture into outer space.

After ten minutes, Jean made her way to the holograph area. As she approached it, a female holograph appeared above a short pedestal and spoke in a smooth, electronic-sounding voice. "Hello, my name is Anta. I can teach you about space exploration, planets, the sun, galaxies, or asteroids. Which one would you like to learn about today?"

Jean waved her arms through the hologram. She couldn't believe how much it looked like a real person. "Planets."

Anta nodded. "Great! I will start with Saturn." A holographic image of the solar system surrounded Jean and a video of Saturn zoomed to the front. Anta explained Saturn's features and provided details about its rings and its place in the solar system. Jean watched the video in awe. Space always fascinated her, but she had seen nothing like this before. The hologram was so realistic that she felt like she was standing on Saturn's surface, gazing up at its stunning rings. *Wow, it would be so cool to be an astronaut. They get to go to other planets.*

As Anta explained the different planets, a strange sensation flowed through Jean's body, causing her to shudder. It seemed as if her legs were melting into the floor. She tried to ignore the feeling and focus on the presentation, but it distracted her. After jiggling her legs, they were normal a few moments later.

When the presentation about planets ended, Jean didn't hear her classmates' usual loud chatter. A chill shot down her spine as she realized she was completely alone. The silence was deafening and the dim lights of the exhibit room flickered ominously, casting eerie shadows on the walls. She swiveled around and her eyes searched the empty exhibit room. Her heart raced as panic set in. She dashed out of the exhibit room, crashing headfirst into a lady. "Sorry," Jean mumbled.

The lady chuckled. "Always watch where you're going, Jean."

Jean glanced up at the lady, who had a huge smile, brown skin, and short, cropped, curly hair. She appeared to be the same age as Jean's teacher and reminded Jean of the military lady who came to the school for career day. *How does she know my name? Maybe I misunderstood. She must not have said Jean.* Jean shrugged before sprinting away to find her classmates.

As Jean looked toward the end of the hall, a kid resembling one of her classmates entered an exhibit. She hurried down the hall and darted in behind him. She was mistaken; the kid she saw wasn't in her class. He was just someone visiting the museum with his parents.

A grassy, piney scent pierced Jean's nostrils. On one side of the room, there was a large sign that read "Plants of the Tundra" hanging above a wide variety of lichen and moss. As Jean studied the vegetation, she read about how the plants survive in such frigid environments. Jean reached a finger toward one plant when she heard laughter. She turned around and saw Amber and Petra standing behind her, pointing and laughing.

"Ooh look, weird girl is playing with moss," Petra said as she shoved past Jean. Amber and Petra laughed. "That's why she gets a new mom every year. She's so weird."

Jean sighed. "Leave me alone," she whined.

"Leave me alone," Petra mocked as she leaned over close to Jean's face. Jean pushed her away. Turning toward Amber, Petra exclaimed, "Did you see what she did?"

"Yeah, she must be tryin' to start a fight. You should tell Ms. Wilkenson."

Petra's nostrils flared as she leaned close to Jean's face. "Is that it, freak? You wanna fight? I'm ready right now."

Jean quickly walked away toward another part of the exhibit that explained the tundra climate. Petra and Amber followed her, but she dashed into a small, unmarked room and pulled the heavy door shut. Jean leaned forward, resting her ear against the door.

"She's in there!" Petra exclaimed.

The door's lock clicked. Jean kept her ear pressed to the door as the muffled sound of Petra and Amber's laughter decreased. Finally, silence filled the air. Relieved, Jean turned the doorknob and pushed on the door, but it didn't budge.

"Help!" Jean banged and kicked the door. "Help me! Can somebody help get me out?" Jean grabbed the door handle and shook it as she slammed her other fist into the door. The door still did not budge, and it seemed as if no one could hear her. Despite the icy air clawing at her skin, her body temperature warmed, eliciting a shudder. She glanced at her arms. There was a yellowish hue to her skin. She collapsed onto the frigid, hard floor, tears streaming down her face. *Why don't they just leave me alone?*

As the tears flowed, Jean thought about her life over the last few years, moving to and from the homes of strangers. Three months ago, she moved into the Anderson's home and they had been so nice, buying her a closet full of clothes and treating her like a member of the family. She'd never met a more loving couple, although she still kept a bag packed with her favorite clothes and toys to be ready in case she had to move. And now, she was stuck alone in a room, wondering if she would ever get out.

Two hours passed, and Jean's stomach rumbled. She glanced toward the door. There was a thermostat perched near the corner which displayed a temperature of 10 degrees Fahrenheit. Jean stood up and yawned as she stared at her fingertips, which appeared a bright red color. A bone-chilling terror coursed through her veins as she frantically banged on the door and screamed. Two minutes later, the door lock clicked. A medium-build maintenance man wearing dark blue overalls peered down at Jean. "What are you doing in there?"

Jean's heart pounded in her chest as if it was trying to escape. She darted out of the room and slammed into a tour guide wearing a purple blazer with blue trousers and high heels. "Sorry," she mumbled.

"This little lady was locked in tundra storage," the maintenance man said.

The tour guide eyeballed Jean. "Oh, no! You poor dear. You feel okay, sweetie? Not too cold?"

Jean shook her head and flexed her fingers. Her skin still tingled with unnatural warmth.

The tour guide grabbed Jean's hand and faced the group she was leading. "Excuse me, everyone. I need to help this young lady find her group. Continue looking around the tundra exhibit, and I will be back shortly." As they exited the exhibit, the tour guide paused. "You're sure you don't need a blanket?"

"No," Jean murmured.

"Well, your hand feels pretty warm. You're not an icicle, so you couldn't have been in there too long, huh? Let's go find your group. Who are you here with?"

"My school."

The tour guide's forehead creased with concern. "Sweetie, what's the name of your school?"

Jean lowered her head. "Explorers Elementary," she said, sniffling.

"Okay, honey, let's go to the information desk and page your group. What grade are you in?"

"Third."

As soon as Jean arrived at the information desk, she saw Ms. Wilkenson and her classmates walking toward them.

"Jean! What did I tell you about staying with your group? Didn't you hear the page? Do you know how much time we had to spend looking for you?" Ms. Wilkenson exclaimed.

"Oh, the poor dear was trapped in the tundra storage room for a short while, but she's not cold and there are no signs of frostbite. It's good we got to her before too long. It looks like she was only in there for a few minutes," the tour guide said, placing a comforting hand on Jean's shoulder.

Ms. Wilkenson shook her head and clicked her tongue. "Everyone, this is why I tell you to remain with your group and to contact a museum worker if you get lost. It's for your own good. There are lots of places where you can get hurt." She pivoted toward Jean. "You'll stay with me from now on. No pizza party for you either."

Petra and Amber giggled as they whispered to each other.

Jean sighed. "But Ms. Wilk—"

"Freak!" Petra yelled, and Jean's classmates roared with laughter.

"Everyone, quiet down. Petra, I better not hear one more word from you. Our next stop is the cafeteria," Ms. Wilkenson said.

After eating, the class gathered by the entrance. Still shaken, Jean stayed close to the teachers as they left the building. As soon as Jean stepped through the door, Petra shoved past, ramming her lanky body into a marble pillar. Jean winced in agony as her arm struck the cold, unyielding marble. "Ow," she cried out, clutching her wrist as a sudden tingling energy surged through her body in response. Her wrist swelled to two times its size.

Ms. Wilkenson rushed to Jean's side. "Somebody alert the museum. Get a medic," she yelled, her hand applying pressure to Jean's bruised and rapidly swelling wrist. "Are you okay? Can you move your hand? Try moving your fingers."

Jean's body tensed as she stared at her wrist without saying a word.

Suddenly, Ms. Wilkenson gasped. Jean's wrist moved, the veins beneath her skin shifting and wriggling, creating the illusion of a miniature marble running through them. Her eyes widened as the wrist returned to its normal size.

Jean stood with her mouth gaping open as she flexed her fingers. Within moments, the bruise and pain had disappeared.

Ms. Wilkenson pressed on Jean's wrist with her thumbs. "Rapid cellular regeneration..." she murmured. "But how?"

Out of nowhere, the military lady Jean saw earlier ran over to Ms. Wilkenson and tapped her on the shoulder. "Excuse me, Ms. Wilkenson, we need to talk," she whispered.

Ms. Wilkenson nodded and the two women strolled away from the students, carrying on a conversation out of Jean's earshot.

Petra gawked, stammering "Freak!" under her breath. Around Jean, the others shrank back in dismay and horror.

Jean trembled, waves of fear and exhilaration crashing over her. *What am I?* The question echoed in her mind. She had no answers, only the bewildering experience of undergoing a rapid metamorphosis into an unknown existence.

3

Family Greetings

Jean sat hunched at her desk in the dorm room, scribbling the answers to her calculus assignment while taking breaks, staring out the window at the morning sun. *Ugh, wake up, brain! Stop daydreaming about soaring through starry skies, and focus! I've read this same calculus equation fifteen times now, and it's still not computing.*

Emmie sat sprawled in the middle of the floor, cutting out photos of recycling bins and gluing them to a poster. Nearby, Carmen stood in front of a mirror, applying mascara to her long lashes.

"I'm all done," Jean said, slamming her notebook shut.

Emmie glanced at Jean. "Yay! Wanna help me finish this poster?"

Jean walked over to Emmie and sat next to her. "Sure. What do you want me to do?"

"Add these stickers around the edges," Emmie said, handing Jean a pack of green stickers.

As Jean opened the stickers, a sudden knock at the door caused her to jump.

Emmie glanced at the door. "Expectin' someone?"

Jean nodded. "No."

"Hey, Carmen, you expectin' someone?"

"Nope."

The knocks continued. "I guess I'll get it." Emmie hopped up and opened the door and Jean's parents were on the other side, their arms overflowing with bags of groceries.

"Good morning. Is Jean here?" Mrs. Anderson asked.

Jean hopped up and ran over to the door. "What are you guys doing here?"

Mrs. Anderson chuckled. "Surprise!" She planted a kiss on Jean's forehead.

"We come bearing gifts of food and snacks," Mr. Anderson exclaimed, raising his arms.

"Here, let me help you," Emmie smiled as she grabbed a couple of bags out of Mr. Anderson's hands. "I'm her roommate, Emmie, and that girl glued to the mirror is the other roommate, Carmen."

"Hi," Carmen said without looking away from the mirror as she puckered her lips and applied lipstick.

Jean grabbed a few bags from Mrs. Anderson and set them on her desk. "Thanks for everything, but I really don't need anything. I still have a ton left over from last week."

Mr. Anderson chuckled. "That's what roommates are for," he said with a wink. "To help you eat your food and snacks."

Mrs. Anderson wrapped her arm around Jean's shoulder and pulled her close. "Besides, we missed you so much. I'll have to try real hard to stop myself from coming here every week."

As the Andersons helped Jean unpack the groceries, her heart swelled. Their visit reminded her of how lucky she was to have them as parents. Suddenly, a fiery tingle erupted on her skin.

Jean tugged her sleeves down, hiding the glowing lesions creeping up her wrists. She edged away from her parents' gazes.

"You feeling okay, honey?" Mr. Anderson asked after Jean grimaced.

"Yeah, I'm good!" She opened her mini-fridge and pretended to be engrossed in organizing its contents to avoid eye contact.

A stabbing pain shot through Jean's abdomen, and she doubled over with a gasp. Mrs. Anderson rushed to her side. Jean waved her off. "Just a little heartburn, no biggie," she said through clenched teeth. Her parents shared a worried look as Jean turned away from them, hiding her glowing, trembling hands.

After enduring the agonizing episode, her parents' suspicion lingered in the air like a heavy fog. She silently cursed the untimely flare-up, her frustration boiling within. Everything had been proceeding seamlessly, like a calm river flowing steadily. But now, her accursed symptoms had resurfaced, disrupting the tranquility. Jean broiled with frustration. Why couldn't she just be normal for one day with her family? Her abnormality had sabotaged everything in her entire life.

4

The Ultimate Test

Although it had only been a month into the semester, Jean couldn't imagine her life without her roommates, who had become her best friends. As the sunrise painted the sky with oranges and yellows, Jean, Emmie, and Carmen hurried to their family history class at the University of Montana. Jean wore a pair of brown hiking boots, blue jeans, and a gray sweater, while Emmie and Carmen wore T-shirts and shorts. As Jean tugged the heavy door to the natural science building, she turned around. "Wait, where's Carmen?"

Emmie shrugged. "Oh, there she is," Emmie said, pointing to Carmen standing near the side of the building, playing with her silky hair as she conversed with a young man. "Who's that cute guy she's talking to?"

Jean glanced at her watch and shrugged. "We only have two minutes."

"Carmen, come on," Emmie yelled. "Girl, Carmen, get over here! Y'all, we're gonna be late."

Carmen hugged the young man she was speaking to and ran to catch up with Emmie and Jean.

"Have you guys started the family tree assignment yet?" Carmen asked.

Emmie scrunched her brows and tipped her head. "Wait, who were you talking to?"

"Oh, that was Mark. We just met, and he told me about a party this weekend. Of course, I expect you to join me. Anyway, about that family tree assignment, I already have a family tree prepared."

Jean sighed. "I don't have information about my biological family, so I guess I'll just research my adoptive family."

Carmen pouted. "I didn't know you were adopted."

Emmie rolled her eyes. "Really, Carmen? Remember her parents? They look nothing like her," she said.

"Oh, right. Anyway, have you been able to get your adoption records? They usually have useful information you can use in your research."

"Uh, no. I don't have any birth information." Emmie and Carmen stared at Jean, waiting for her to continue. "It's a long story," Jean said, shifting in her seat. *They really don't need to know my mother abandoned me. I mean, it's not a big deal, but it's none of their business. Carmen probably wouldn't care too much and Emmie… well, I don't know how she would feel, but I don't want her to feel sorry for me.*

"Well, ladies, we are officially late," Emmie exclaimed as they entered the classroom filled with auditorium-style seating.

"Thank God for air conditioning. I thought I was going to melt. Can you believe how humid it is out there?" Carmen said as she quickly wrapped her long blonde hair into a bun and plopped down into the nearest empty seat.

Emmie giggled. "Ya'll better get used to it. With all this global warming, we'll be part of the tropics in a few short years."

"I haven't even noticed," Jean said.

Emmie slid a notebook out of her backpack and fanned herself with it. "How could you not notice? We've been in a heat wave all week."

Jean pointed toward the front of the room. "Who's that man?"

"I'm not sure. Oh, wait." Carmen pulled out a copy of the course syllabus. "Today is DNA testing day. It looks like you'll get some info about your bio family."

"Yeah." Jean slumped down in her chair. *I need to learn about my heritage, but how will Mom and Dad feel? I don't want to hurt their feelings. And what type of mother dumps her newborn baby in a park? What if my biological parents are terrible people? What if they're criminals? If I came from a terrible family, does that mean I'm terrible too? Is it better to know my genetic background? I have great parents. Do I really need to meet by bio parents? Strange things have been happening and they may have answers, but at what cost?*

A seven-foot-tall man with stark white hair and light blue eyes stood behind a podium and tapped the microphone. "Good morning, ladies and gentlemen. My name is Dr. Krenik. I am the head of the genealogy department. Today, we are going to administer a DNA test. Although the test is not mandatory, it will help you greatly with your family history assignments. Don't worry. There is no pain involved." Dr. Krenik chuckled.

"We will simply swab your mouth and insert the results into the machine on the table over there," Dr. Krenik said as he pointed toward the long table behind him. "The machine will analyze your DNA on the swab and print a report in a few quick minutes. That report will contain information about where your ancestors came from. The attached computer will upload your DNA information to an international database and compile a list of other DNA test takers who share DNA with you. Years ago, you would have needed to wait months for this type of information. Now, we can provide immediate results. Any questions?"

Loud chatter filled the room. Many students spoke about the different places where their ancestors came from based on information from their parents.

"Okay, hearing no questions, I would like to introduce my assistant, Ziva Mooley, standing to my right. She will swab your cheek and enter your information into the DNA analyzer. We'll start by having everyone in row one taking the test to line up near the machine."

Ziva glanced at her watch. "Okay, let's get started, everyone. Row one," she said, waving her arm forward.

A young man named Jacob approached Jean, Emmie, and Carmen. "We're having a contest. You write the locations where your ancestors came from and the percentages. Whoever is the most accurate wins the pot. $1 to enter."

"I'll pass," Jean said.

"Are you sure? The more people who enter, the more you can win," Jacob said, fanning the dollar bills in his hand.

Emmie pulled a dollar from the front pocket of her backpack and handed it to Jacob. "She doesn't know anything about her family, but I'll enter."

Jean rolled her eyes. "Gee, thanks for making me feel so much better, Emmie," she groaned. "This assignment is going to suck."

"Girl, I get it. I moved around so much, I barely know most of my family. Hey, after today, you'll know something about yours," Emmie said.

"If I decide to take the test," Jean huffed. *What do you do when you want to know something and don't want to know at the same time?*

"Girl, you need to take the test. Besides, how else are you gonna complete the assignment?"

Of course, Emmie's right. I have no choice but to complete the assignment if I want to pass this class. "I'm going to ask the professor." Jean strolled up to Professor Higgins, who stood at the side of the room while Dr. Krenik answered questions. "Excuse me, Professor Higgins?"

Professor Higgins turned, peering over her wire-frame glasses. "Yes?"

Jean rubbed her palms against her pant legs. "Um, I have a question about the family history assignment. I'm adopted, and I was wondering if it's possible for me to just complete the assignment for my adoptive family's tree. I'm not sure if I want to do the test."

"One moment." Professor Higgins walked over to the podium. "Excuse me, Doctor. I just want to make an announcement to the class. Okay, everyone, your family tree can be for anyone you consider family. That includes an adoptive family. However, you get ten bonus points for taking the DNA test and the ethnicity research portion of the assignment is more for your benefit. The best way to learn your ethnicity is to do the DNA test. Now, you are free to research any ethnicities you want, but the best way to get the most out of the family history class is to learn as much as possible about yourself." Professor Higgins warmly smiled at Jean.

Jean scampered back to her seat.

"So, you're gonna take it?" Emmie asked.

"I'm not sure." Jean sighed. "I'm still deciding."

Emmie leaned in, her eyes sparkling with excitement. "Do it! This is your chance to learn about your heritage, plus you get bonus points. It's a win-win," she exclaimed.

"I already know a lot about my heritage," Carmen said, her voice filled with confidence. "My grandmother researched my family tree, so it's an easy A for me."

Jean furrowed her brow. "You're so lucky. What do you know about your family?"

"Well," Carmen began, her tone slightly hushed, as if revealing a secret. "One of my grandmothers immigrated from Ireland, but her father is Russian. My other grandmother is Native American. Let me know if you have questions about genealogy. I learned a lot from my grandmother."

"Hey, Jean, wouldn't it be funny if we found out we're related? I went to school with a guy whose mother found out she was her co-worker's sibling after taking the DNA test," Emmie said.

"No offense, Emmie, but I seriously doubt we're related. Don't get me wrong, I would love having you as a sister, but I think it's safe to say we're not related."

"Well, you'll never know who you're related to if you don't take the test," Emmie said in a sing-song voice.

Jean let out a resigned sigh. "Ugh, fine. I'll do it. But when it says you are not my sister, you owe me a latte," she said, giggling.

Emmie's eyes widened as her mouth curled into a gentle smile. "Ya won't be sorry. I'm so excited for you!"

"Okay, everyone in row 23 who's taking the test can line up in the front," Professor Higgins instructed.

Carmen hopped up. "That's us. Are you ready?"

Jean froze. "No."

Emmie wrapped her arm around Jean's shoulder. "Come on. It'll be fun."

As Jean strolled to the front of the room, her heart raced. There was an exit door near the front and she stared at it, wondering if she should leave. "Well, you go first."

Emmie stepped forward. "Carmen, let's show Jean how easy it is."

"I'll go first." Carmen hopped in front of Emmie and sashayed over to Ziva. After Ziva swabbed the inside of her cheeks, she instructed Carmen to sit in the chair next to the DNA analyzer while the machine processed her results. Carmen sat down and smiled at Jean. "See, that wasn't too bad. All you need to do is get swabbed and sit next to the machine. It doesn't hurt at all."

After ten minutes, Dr. Krenik pulled Carmen's results from the analyzer and handed them to Ziva. Ziva showed the report to Carmen and explained how her DNA showed she had ancestors from Ireland, Greece, and Italy. After Emmie took the test and got her results, Jean slowly approached Ziva to be swabbed. Her entire body shook with a mix of nervousness and excitement.

Ziva inserted the swab into Jean's mouth. "Hold still. I'm not gonna be able to get your results if you keep moving around like that."

Jean froze. She didn't realize she had been moving. After being swabbed, she sat and waited. Within a few minutes, Ziva pulled the printed copy of Jean's results and approached Jean.

"Okay, your report shows your DNA is from the following regions: 22% Nigeria, 5% Southern Philippines, 5% Scotland, 5% Norway, 1% Wales, 62% un... Wait, that's weird." Ziva frowned as she stared at the report. "Hmm, why does it say that?"

Jean scrunched her brows and stood. "Is something wrong?"

"It's just that I never saw this before. Sometimes, we see a tiny percentage as undetermined, but your report has an exorbitant amount."

Jean stared intently at Ziva, her eyebrows furrowing in confusion. The fluorescent lights overhead hummed softly, casting a sterile glow across the room. The faint scent of antiseptic lingered in the air as Ziva's fingers fervently tapped the machine's buttons.

"Um, Dr. Krenik, can you come here, please?" Ziva's voice cut through the quiet room, breaking the silence. Her footsteps echoed softly as she strolled toward Dr. Krenik, the sound of her shoes against the linoleum floor.

Dr. Krenik, a tall figure with a confident stride, sauntered over to Ziva, his white lab coat swaying slightly. The sound of his footsteps merged with Ziva's, creating a symphony of anticipation.

"What's going on?" Dr. Krenik inquired, his deep voice resonating through the room.

Ziva held up the report and flipped through it. The crisp pages rustled in her hands, the sound almost drowning out the machine's soft hum.

"It didn't analyze all her DNA," Ziva explained, her voice tinged with concern. "Is it broken?"

Dr. Krenik reached out and snatched the test results from Ziva's hand. His eyes swiftly scanned the report. "Whose test is this?"

Ziva pointed toward Jean, her finger trembling slightly with unease.

Dr. Krenik studied the results. After reading them, his eyes met Jean's with an intense stare. Unnerved, Jean turned her back to him.

"I can't believe it. After all these years ... I finally found one of the missing..." Dr. Krenik walked toward Jean and waved his arm. "Young lady..."

Carmen looked up after reviewing her test results and edged closer to Jean. "What's going on?"

"I don't know. I think I'm just gonna leave. This was a bad idea," Jean said, a shiver running down her spine. She flung her backpack hastily over her shoulder and strolled toward the exit, eager to escape his penetrating gaze. As Jean reached for the door handle, there was a sudden vise-like grip on her wrist. Heart racing, she whirled around to find Dr. Krenik clutching her arm, his face mere inches from hers.

"Let go of me," Jean cried out as she tried to pry his fingers off her arm. *Why is he grabbing me? I need to get out of here.* Jean gasped as her breathing intensified. She looked around frantically before spotting Professor Higgins. "He won't let go of me," Jean cried out, her voice trembling.

Professor Higgins darted over to Jean.

"He won't let go," Jean said as she struggled to pull Dr. Krenik's hand off her wrist.

"Let go of her! Release her right now!" Professor Higgins grabbed Dr. Krenik's hand and pried it off Jean's wrist.

Loud chatter filled the room. Jean staggered toward the door and ran out of the auditorium, rubbing her wrist. She could still feel the imprint of Krenik's grip burning into her skin. Carmen and Emmie followed closely behind her.

"OMG, what was that about?" Emmie asked.

"I have no idea." Jean looked over her shoulder at her classroom door and saw Dr. Krenik staring at her through the door's glass window. "Let's just get out of here. That guy really creeps me out."

Carmen stuffed her test results into her backpack. "Do you want me to go see what that was about? I can talk to the professor."

Jean shook her head and took a deep inhale. "No. I just wanna leave. My hands are still shaking."

"When's your next class?" Emmie asked.

Jean sighed and glanced at her watch. "In two hours. I think I'm going back to the dorm until then. I need time to decompress."

5

Seeking Answers

After Jean left, Emmie stood outside the Natural Science building next to Carmen, squinting against the harsh mid-morning sun. Her stomach churned as she watched Jean's figure grow smaller as she scurried across campus.

Emmie scrunched her brows. "I'm worried. You think she's okay?"

"She probably just needs some alone time." Carmen glanced at her phone. "I think I'm going to grab some coffee at the Student Union before my next class. Do you want to come?"

Emmie sighed. "Maybe I should check on Jean."

"Wasn't that doctor creepy?" Carmen asked, scrunching her face. "I wonder what that was about."

Emmie shivered as the memory of his icy stare sent chills down her spine. As someone who barely knew family members beyond her parents, she couldn't help but sympathize with Jean's plight. "Yeah, I feel so bad for Jean. This was her chance to get information about her DNA and they messed up her test." Emmie's heart ached for her friend, remembering her own childhood loneliness. As a military kid, she had moved every two years, never settling long enough to build lasting bonds. She craved an enduring sense of belonging. The test failure had crushed Jean's hopes of anchoring herself with blood ties after floating adrift for so long.

"Or perhaps it was Jean who messed up the test," Carmen suggested. Her gaze wandered away, avoiding Emmie's probing eyes. "You have to consider the possibility. She's always been a little different, hasn't she? Maybe there's something peculiar in her DNA that disrupted the machine. And that doctor, well, he must have sensed something was amiss."

"What do ya mean, different? She seems perfectly nice to me. Sometimes she seems a little timid, but I don't think she's that different from anyone else."

Carmen held up her hands in mock surrender. "Okay, forget I said anything," she said, shoving open the Student Union door.

"Actually, I'll catch up with you later. I'm gonna head back to the Natural Science building to see if I can talk to Dr. Krenik," Emmie said. She had to talk to that doctor and find out what really went wrong. She couldn't let Jean lose this chance. Everyone deserved answers about where they came from and the family waiting for them.

Carmen shrugged as she tapped an app on her cellphone. "If you say so."

Emmie's mind raced as she jogged across campus. She had to be tactful, but also persistent when she questioned the doctor. *I know, I'm gonna ask him what was wrong with her test and if she can take it again. Wait, he was acting really creepy, so I'll need to make sure I keep my distance.*

As Emmie headed toward the classroom, she saw Dr. Krenik standing in the hallway talking on his cellphone. After he stopped talking and slipped his phone into his pocket, she approached him. "Excuse me, Dr. Krenik. I was hopin' we could talk more about my friend Jean's test results. They were undetermined."

The doctor's eyes narrowed, his expression unreadable. "Where is she?"

"Uh, she left. Um, is it possible for…"

"Young lady, I cannot discuss her test with you. That's confidential information. Where is she?"

"I don't know. Look, is there any way she can take the test again?"

"We are not doing retakes at this time." Dr. Krenik turned abruptly and walked away.

Emmie's shoulders slumped in defeat. There was definitely something strange happening, but getting answers out of the stern doctor seemed unlikely. She had to keep digging. *Maybe I'll talk to the professor about what happened or buy Jean a commercial DNA kit. I won't stop until this is resolved.*

6

Revelations

J ean sat on her bed, leaning against the back wall as she thought about the day's events. *Is something wrong with my DNA? Maybe instead of worrying about a DNA test, I need to go to a doctor.* Jean took a deep breath and closed her eyes. *People inherit all types of things from their parents. I don't feel as if something is wrong. Who am I kidding? I know something's wrong. What if I inherited a terrible disease and I'm slowly dying without realizing it? This is crazy. I had a chance to get information about my bio family and the machine broke. Yeah, that must be it. The machine couldn't read my DNA because it broke. Should I see if I can take the test again or just forget about it?*

Jean glanced at her watch. *Oops, I'm late for class.* She hopped up and jogged across campus to her calculus class. As she crossed a campus parking lot, she saw Ziva loading the DNA analyzer into a black van. Her breath stuck in her throat and her palms grew sweaty. She took a deep breath and approached Ziva. "Excuse me, do you remember me from the DNA testing?" Her voice was shakier than she had intended.

Ziva turned, her piercing gaze sending a chill down Jean's spine. "Oh, yeah. How could I forget you?" she mumbled as she shoved the analyzer further into the back of the van. "I don't know what was going on with that old man. He should have retired a long time ago. I'm so glad I won't have to deal with him anymore."

"Right, um, I never received my report," Jean's voice continued to tremble.

Ziva's eyes narrowed as she huffed. "What?"

Jean took a deep breath and straightened her posture. "I never received my DNA report. You said something about it being undetermined."

Ziva looked Jean up and down.

"Can you give me my report?"

"If you insist." Ziva reached into a box in the van and pulled out a manila file folder. "I take no responsibility for the incomplete information on your report." She shoved the folder toward Jean. "I assume this is what you're looking for. Your test results are in this file, along with a list of people who took the test and share DNA with you."

"Thank you," Jean said as she stuffed the results into her backpack.

"You can leave now," Ziva said as she waved Jean away. She climbed into the van, slammed the door, and quickly backed up before speeding away.

"Right." Jean strolled to her calculus class, wondering about the incomplete information in her report. Other students she passed seemed so carefree as they chatted with each other and laughed or walked with determination. *I didn't hear her say anything about undetermined DNA to any of the other students. What's wrong with me? Why am I so different? What does undetermined even mean? Maybe I should see if I can do another DNA test. No, they took the machine away.* Jean sighed. *I don't know, maybe I should just skip calculus.* Jean swung her bag off her shoulder, almost hitting another student. The other student gasped. "Sorry, I'm so sorry," Jean said. She put the backpack back on her shoulders and entered her class, sitting in the seat closest to the door.

Ugh, why did I come here? I can't concentrate. Jean tapped her fingers on the desk until she saw the professor looking at her. She unzipped her bag, pulled the test out, then slipped it back in. *I'll wait. I need to focus on class. His voice is so monotone. I'll be glad when this is over. Oh, I just thought of something. Although the test was undetermined, it did have some information.* She lifted up the flap of her bag. *No, I'll wait. Let me try to concentrate on class and pray I don't fall asleep.*

After class, Jean met up with Emmie and Carmen at the Student Union in a lounge area with round tables in the center of the room. Meeting at the Student Union after classes had become their daily routine. Jean loved meeting there to discuss the day's events while people-watching. She often grabbed a snack and bottle of water from the vending machine before finding a seat at the only empty table. Ten minutes after sitting down, Carmen and Emmie approached Jean.

Jean waved at them, smiling. "Hey, guys."

Carmen plopped down into the chair closest to Jean. "I've been waiting all day for this."

"For what?" Jean asked.

"Oh, don't act like you don't know."

Jean scrunched her eyebrows as she bit into a cheese puff. "Huh?"

"What happened with your DNA test?"

Emmie piped up. "Yeah, Jean. What happened? Why did that doctor grab you like that?"

"I don't know, but I saw that lady, you know, the assistant. Anyway, she was loading the machine into a van when I was on my way to class and I asked her for my test report."

Carmen raised a brow. "Well, what did it say?"

Jean slumped down in her chair. "I don't know. I haven't looked at it yet. I'm almost scared to look."

Emmie and Carmen glanced at each other with a shocked expression.

"Don't you want to know?" Emmie scooted her chair closer to Jean.

"Yeah, but..." *How should I tell them I want to know, but I also don't want to know. Does that even make sense?*

"Okay," Carmen said, tapping her skinny, manicured finger on the table. "Hand it over."

Jean slowly unzipped her backpack, pulled out the file folder, and tossed it onto the table.

Carmen snatched up the folder and opened it. "Okay ladies, let's learn about Jean." Carmen silently read the report and suddenly gasped.

Carmen slid the report across the table to Jean. "There's a list of people you share DNA with. They're your biological family."

Jean flipped through the pages, glancing at the list of names and their corresponding percentage of shared DNA. *Novar, 1086 cM, Susan Cartwright, 786 cM.* She smiled as a rush of excitement shot through her body. Some names had photos next to them. Jean squinted as she looked to see if she resembled any of the matches. "They're my family." After all these years, she finally got to learn about her family. She was able to see what they looked like and where they came from. After scanning some of the family names, she saw a section called "Ethnic Origins" and read a word she had never seen before. "Look at this. The doctor's assistant mentioned something that was undetermined, but it says potential..." Jean picked up the report and held it close to her eyes.

"What? Potential what?" Emmie stood, walked behind Jean, and peered over her shoulder.

"Potential Xeno ethnicity," Jean muttered with a quizzical look in her eyes. Jean stared at the crumpled lab report, reading the words "potential Xeno ethnicity" over and over. Xeno. The unfamiliar term gnawed at her mind.

"I never heard of that country," Carmen stated as she slipped a mirror out of her bag and started touching up her lipstick.

Emmie's eyes widened. "Xeno? As in ... *alien*?"

Carmen giggled. "Seriously, Emmie! Quit joking!"

"I'm not kidding. Xeno means alien."

Jean looked up from the report. "You mean illegal alien?"

Emmie tilted her head forward and peered over her wire-rim glasses. "I mean alien as in outer space alien. You know, the kind from another planet."

"Jean's an alien from outer space?" Carmen squealed.

A group of football players wearing grass-stained jerseys chatted and joked while seated at a long table nearby. After Carmen's statement, they quieted down. A broad-shouldered player with short red hair and a mischievous glint in his eyes called out, "Alien? Jean's an alien?" He elbowed the teammate next to him, a tall and muscular young man with dark skin, eliciting laughter from the other teammates.

"Hey, which one of you is Jean?" the red-haired player continued, scanning the cafeteria with curiosity. His teammates joined in, their eyes searching the room.

Jean's skin prickled with the sensation of being under scrutiny. She stuffed the test results into her backpack and hopped up from the table. She hurried out the door and headed toward her dorm. The hairs on the back of her neck stood up as the distinct sensation of someone following her emerged. She glanced over her shoulder at Carmen and Emmie. "Not cool bringing up those memories, guys."

"Jean, wait! Slow down. What memories?" Carmen asked.

"Jean, I'm sorry. But you're the one who said Xeno. I just told you what it means," Emmie exclaimed.

Jean stopped walking and turned to face Emmie. "The report says undetermined. You called me an alien."

Emmie huffed. "Your report says possible Xeno origin. Xeno means alien. Don't blame me for what your report says."

"It's not possible. There's no such thing as aliens. Anyway, it was probably a mistake. That dumb machine was probably broken." Jean swiveled around and continued walking. *Aliens. Hmm, who would think ... wait ... what if I'm really an alien?! That would explain why I never fit in or understood humans. Haha, yeah right. I know I have a weird imagination, but that's just crazy.*

The ground seemed to drop from beneath Jean's feet. Xeno? She gripped her arms, digging her nails in to feel something solid, anything to anchor her. A Xeno? Bile burned the back of her throat. Flashes of news footage bombarded her—random UFO sightings, aliens abducting humans for twisted experiments, those chilling black eyes staring out defiantly.

Her stomach roiled and twisted. *How can I be one of them?* She searched her murky childhood memories, seeking any hint, desperate for an alternate explanation. But many memories lent support to her alien ancestry. *Have I been spending my whole life in denial?*

Jean plopped down onto a wooden bench and squeezed her eyes shut, pressing the heels of her palms against them until bursting colors gave way to darkness. She focused on steadying her breaths, in and out, slow and deep. It did nothing to steady her stampeding heart or untwist the knots coiling through her insides.

Who am I now? Do I even know myself at all? Xenos are the enemy ... aren't they? No, I am Jean. My actions define me, not my blood. With stubborn determination, she clung to the tattered remains of her identity, afraid to examine it too closely in case it disintegrated in her hands. She had to believe that still meant something, even if the world disagreed.

Carmen tapped Jean on her shoulder. "Jean, let me see your report? I just want to see something."

Jean sighed as she yanked the report out of her bag and handed it to Carmen.

Carmen perused the report's contents and looked up at Jean with widened eyes. "Jean, did you read this entire report?"

Jean shrugged. "Well, I didn't read all of it yet. Why? What's wrong?"

Carmen pointed at a page on the report. "It names your birth father. His name is Azon. It doesn't give a last name."

Jean's heart skipped a beat, and she froze as she glanced at Emmie. "How..."

Carmen looked down at the report again. "And there's something else. It looks like you also have a brother. The report says he's a half-sibling. It gives more information about him. It says his name is Kale Daniels, and he lives in Seattle, in the Capitol Hill district." Carmen handed the report back to Jean. "See, the information is there," Carmen said as she pointed to his profile in the report.

Jean stared at the report, which now had crumpled pages from being stuffed in her bag. "I guess I was so bothered by the undetermined information, I forgot to read the rest," Jean mumbled. After 18 years, this sheet of paper finally connected her to the missing pieces of her origins.

"Azon." Her heartbeat quickened as she said his name, wondering what he looked like and who he was. Did he know about her? Did he wonder about the baby daughter he never got to raise?

Further down the report, another name leaped off the page—Kale Daniels. Her brother. Jean broke into a wide, tearful smile. She had a brother! A cascade of questions flooded her mind. Was he older or younger? What was he like? What traits did they share? She thought about what it would be like to meet her family. Jean imagined showing up on their doorstep, introducing herself, and seeing her own smile reflected in their faces. The fantasy filled her with exhilaration. She became increasingly excited about the possibility of meeting them. "I'm going to do it."

Emmie and Carmen looked at each other. "Do what?" they said simultaneously and giggled, realizing they had the same thought.

Jean grinned. "Okay, I know it's crazy, but I'm going to do it. I'm going to Seattle. I'm gonna meet my brother." Jean's smile seemed to fill her entire face. She pulled out her phone and started searching for Kale Daniels online. "I'm leaving tonight."

Carmen's mouth gaped open. "Uh, are you sure that's a good idea? I mean, what if that's not really his name? What if he's some sort of psychopath?"

Emmie scrunched her face. "Or a serial killer," she chimed in.

"Guys, this is my one chance to meet family. Look, I think I found him. It says he owns a tattoo parlor. That's pretty cool."

Carmen shook her head. "I'm not saying you shouldn't reach out to him. Maybe call him on the phone or email him. I mean, it would be pretty creepy if some unknown relative just showed up at my front door. I don't know what I would do."

Jean sighed. "You don't understand. I'm his *sister*. Why would he be creeped out by me? Besides, I'm going to meet him in a public place. Maybe I'll tell him I want a tattoo."

"You really want a tattoo?" Emmie asked.

"No ... I don't know. Maybe."

"I think you should take the time to think about this. At least go with another person. If you wait until Saturday, I'll ride there with you. Emmie will come too. Right, Emmie?"

Emmie brushed her palms together and flashed a huge smile. "Ya'll, a roomie road trip sounds like fun. I'll bring the snacks and we can play car games. If ya can wait until the weekend..."

"I'm just too excited to wait. Besides, I have a meeting on Saturday." Jean looked up from her phone. Carmen was staring at her with a horrified look on her face. "Don't worry. I'll keep you guys updated. Hey, I'll even share my GPS with you so you'll know where I am at all times."

"I don't feel good about this. I mean, how would you feel if things were reversed? What if an unknown relative showed up here after getting the DNA results?" Carmen asked.

"I'm not sure how I would feel, but I believe I might think it was cool to meet a biological relative."

"And, at least one of your roommates would welcome that relative with open arms." Emmie wrapped her arm around Carmen's shoulder. "Carmen, she said she'll share her location. She'll be okay. This is her chance to meet family. And if she goes missin' or somethin' bad happens, at least we'll know where to look."

Carmen sighed. "When are you leaving?"

"I'm not sure. I want to look into something before I leave."

When Jean returned to her room, she spent hours scouring online genealogical archives and reading about aliens. Names of her DNA matches swirled in her head as she pored over census records and funeral ledgers, determined to unravel her genetic puzzle. She couldn't think about her studies until she uncovered answers about her heritage. Only then could she still the relentless questions echoing through her mind: Where did she come from? Who were her people? What was she? And why did her mother abandon her?

She searched through her closet, trying to decide which bag she should take on her journey. After finding a large duffel bag, she tossed it onto her bed and sat down, fingering her test printout. She thought about the number of times she moved with everything she owned stuffed into a small, raggedy duffel bag. She leaned against the wall and daydreamed as she thought about her thirteenth birthday. It was a special moment for her. Her parents entered the room singing "Happy Birthday." Mr. Anderson tapped the alarm clock as Mrs. Anderson hugged Jean and sat on the edge of her bed.

Mr. Anderson grinned. "Welcome to the teenage years. How does it feel?"

"I don't know. I guess I feel the same way I felt yesterday," Jean said as she wiped her eyes.

"Well, we have a surprise. There's something we've been working on for a while now and we finally have a court date."

"A court date?"

Mr. Anderson smiled. "That's right, baby girl." He turned toward Mrs. Anderson. "Do you want to tell her, or should I?"

"Ooh, I can't wait any longer," Mrs. Anderson said. "Remember when we talked about making you a permanent part of our family?"

"Yeah."

"Well, it's finally gonna happen. You are officially going to be an Anderson. We have an adoption hearing scheduled next week."

Jean smiled. "I can't wait!" Finally, she was going to be part of a family. She never had to worry about being taken away and placed with a different family again. This was the best birthday. Jean peeked at the small mirror on her nightstand and grinned. Although she was going to be adopted, her grin reminded her of Mrs. Anderson's grin. Nothing else looked the same. Jean wondered what others would think once they became a real family. She was so different from the Andersons. "Um, Mom, am I old enough now?"

"Old enough for what?"

"Old enough to find out what happened. I mean why am I not with the mom who had me?"

Mrs. Anderson sighed and glanced at Mr. Anderson. Mr. Anderson nodded. "Well, I guess it's time for you to know something." Mrs. Anderson paused. "Unfortunately, we don't have much information about your biological family. No one knows who your birth mother is. The only thing we know is that a young man found you alone in a park. You were so tiny that you couldn't have been more than a few hours old. I'll be right back." Mrs. Anderson left the room and returned carrying a neatly folded piece of paper. "You were wrapped in a blanket with this note," she said, handing it to Jean.

Jean held the note between her fingers for a minute and took a deep breath before carefully unfolding it. "Please take care of my beautiful baby and give her a wonderful life. To my Jean, please know I will always look after you from afar. From distant soils, you bear unseen potential. Do not let the fear of others dim your brightness within. Until we meet again."

Mrs. Anderson wrapped her arm around Jean's shoulder. "I'm so sorry. I wish I could tell you more. Everyone deserves to know where they came from."

"That's okay. You're my family now."

After thinking about her thirteenth birthday, Jean smiled. Her parents' love warmed her heart. How would they feel about her search for her biological family? She never wanted them to feel as if they were being replaced by her biological parents. *They will always be my family. I just want answers.* Jean paced around her dorm room, her trembling fingers gripping her cellphone. Her heart rate leaped higher as she considered telling her parents about finding information about her brother. Would they be worried?

Jean chewed her lip anxiously. Beneath her nervousness, a current of excitement surged through her veins. She couldn't wait to tell her mother and took a deep breath as she dialed her number.

"Hi honey. How's everything?"

"Pretty good. I really like my roommates and my classes are going well. Guess what? I found out I have a brother."

After a brief silence, Mrs. Anderson let out an elated gasp. "Oh my, you found your birth family?"

"Yeah, well, we took a DNA test in one of my classes and they gave us a list of people who share DNA with us. My list included a brother who lives in Seattle."

"Ooh, that's great! I'm so happy for you. Maybe you'll get to meet him one day. You know, your dad and I have always been supportive of you finding your biological family."

"I know. Actually, I'm thinking about driving to Seattle to meet him," Jean said, her heart pounding in anticipation of her mother's reaction.

A stunned silence followed. Jean gripped the phone tighter, palms sweating.

"You're driving all alone to Seattle?" Mrs. Anderson asked, her voice rising in alarm.

Jean released a deep sigh as her shoulders tensed. "I know what you're thinking, but I've been waiting my whole life to learn about my family. I mean, you're my family, too. But I have questions that only they can answer."

"Honey, please be reasonable. Your dad and I can go with you next weekend."

"That doesn't work as well for my schedule. I was actually thinking about going this evening."

Mrs. Anderson gasped. "Why so soon? We can't make it tonight."

"Tomorrow is my free day. I don't plan to stay long. I just want to go there for the day, meet him, and then return home."

"Wouldn't the weekend be better?"

"I have a meeting for a group project on Saturday."

"I still think your father and I should go with you," her mom pleaded. "It's just not safe traveling so far alone."

"Mom, I know you're worried, but this is really important to me. I can do this by myself. Please try to understand."

"But honey..."

"This is more than just meeting my brother. It's about discovering who I am and where I come from. I need to do this myself. I promise I'll be careful. I'll call you as soon as I get there." Jean held her breath, waiting for her mother's response.

Mrs. Anderson let out a resigned sigh. "Okay, honey. I can see how much this means to you. Please call me the moment you get there safely. You know how I worry about you."

After finishing her assignment, Jean grabbed her tote bag and headed to her car. She strolled across the parking lot, rummaging in her bag, searching for her car key fob. She was so lost in thought about finding her brother that she didn't notice the lone figure standing near her car until she hit the unlock button. The headlights flashed, illuminating the man's face. Jean froze. It was Dr. Krenik.

Before Jean could react, Dr. Krenik took a couple of steps toward her. "Wait, I need to talk to you."

Jean's heart hammered against her ribs. What was he doing here? How did he know which car belonged to her? She wanted to run, but her legs were frozen in place.

Dr. Krenik inched closer. There was an unsettling urgency in his voice. "It's very important that you listen to me. Your test results—there's something you must know."

Panic flooded Jean's veins. She fumbled with the door handle before pulling it open and diving inside. Her tires squealed as she peeled out of the parking space. As she sped away, she tightly gripped the steering wheel and continuously checked the rearview mirror until Dr. Krenik's figure shrunk out of view. What did he want from her? And why did it seem like he refused to stop until he got it?

Jean's pulse jumped as she sped into the night, with Dr. Krenik's cryptic warning plaguing her thoughts. She hoped the trip to see her brother would provide answers, but it left her with troubling questions instead.

7

Twisted Highway

J ean sped toward the ramp to Interstate 90 and hopped onto the freeway toward Seattle. An orange hue filled the sky as the sun began to set. Fortunately, there weren't many cars on the highway, so Jean felt she should be able to make good progress before it got too dark. She planned to find a hotel at the first sign of exhaustion.

After a half hour, Jean's phone rang. "Answer call. Hello," Jean said.

Carmen's voice came through the car's speaker. "Hey. Where are you?"

"Hi Carmen. Remember, I told you? I'm heading to Seattle to find my brother."

"I really think you should wait. Are you sure you don't want to call first? It's not too late to change your mind."

Jean sighed. "Nope, I already decided."

"Hey, Jean, I'm here too," Emmie said. "Carmen has you on speakerphone. I agree with her. If you wait until the weekend, we can go with you. Come back and we'll start makin' plans."

"I'm already halfway there. Anyway, I think it will be better if I go alone. I don't want to scare him away if a group of us shows up."

"You know I'm excited about you meetin' your brother, but it's safer to travel in groups," Emmie exclaimed.

"You sound like my mom."

"Your mom will totally kill us if anything bad happens to you. Remember what she said? She told us to look after her baby and if anything happened, she would come after us," Carmen said.

Jean giggled. "I'm pretty sure she was joking."

"Yeah, well, call us as soon as you get there. If we don't hear from you, we'll come looking for you."

"Or, we'll call the police," Emmie quipped.

"Guys, I'll be okay! I promise." Jean chuckled. "And I gave you access to my GPS information. You should have received an email. Plus, I'll call as soon as I reach Seattle."

Emmie chuckled. "Girl, you better!"

After ending the call, Jean turned her attention to the road. She had little experience driving when it was very dark. To calm her nerves, she blasted music while the darkening sky fell over the flat expanse of the countryside lining the freeway.

Suddenly, a bright light flashed in her rearview mirror. Jean blinked. *Ugh, turn off the bright lights, idiot.* BOOM. She gasped as something pummeled into her car like a thunderbolt, sending her into a dizzying spiral. Struggling to regain control of the car, Jean's fingers squeezed the steering wheel as her heart pounded against her chest and her entire body tensed. Squealing tires pierced her ears before her front bumper crumpled against the divider with a sickening crunch. The airbag exploded in her face like a firm pillow to the nose. Teetering and toppling, her car rolled upside down and skidded with an agonizing, metallic screech, landing with a bone-jarring thud in a ditch.

Jean's entire body melted into her seat. She peeled her eyes open and wriggled her arms and legs. They were soft and wobbly, as if they were gelatin. After a couple of minutes, they stiffened. Fortunately, Jean only felt a little sore and attempted to climb out of her car. As she struggled to unfasten her seat belt, a bright light shone in her window. *Oh good, someone is here to help me.* Jean squinted as the light intensified. Two dark SUVs pulled to a halt a short distance away from her car.

The sound of multiple sets of heavy boots pounding the gravel intensified as several men approached Jean's car. One man crouched down next to Jean's car and peered into her window. The harsh shadow of the headlights behind him made seeing his face difficult, but Jean caught a glimpse of his hard, green eyes. She opened her mouth to speak, but the man quickly turned away before she could say anything.

"Get her out of there," the man yelled.

Another man stepped forward. "Are you sure we should move her? Movement can make some injuries worse." *Who is that?* The voice sounded familiar, but she didn't know why. The man crouched down in front of Jean. "Don't worry, we'll get you out."

"Get out of the way, old man. If what you said is true, it'll take more than a tumble to break her bones." The man motioned to some of the other men standing nearby. "You two work on getting her out. Gerard, see if there's a saw or something in the trunk we can use to cut her out."

The man with the familiar-sounding voice stepped away and made a phone call.

"I got somethin' to cut the belt." A burly man reached into the SUV's glove compartment and pulled out a seat belt cutter. "Don't move." He reached through the broken window and sliced her seat belt in several places.

Jean breathed a sigh of relief after being released from the belt's tight hold. *What did he mean about it taking more than a tumble to break my bones?*

Two other men came and pulled Jean out of the car and laid her on the ground.

Jean sat up, leaning on her elbows. She was relieved to be alive and out of her mangled vehicle. As she looked around, a SUV with a crumpled front bumper sat parked a few feet from her car. Fogginess filled her head. *I'm supposed to exchange information. Something doesn't feel right.*

The man with the green eyes crouched down in front of Jean and studied her face for what seemed like forever.

Jean cleared her throat. "Hello?"

"You're Jean Anderson, aren't you?"

Jean's throat was unusually dry. "Uh..."

The man with the familiar-sounding voice returned. "Is she okay? This wasn't what we discussed. Hurry, get her out of there."

Jean turned toward the man who stepped forward. His voice was familiar. She looked up and recognized the creepy man, Dr. Krenik.

The green-eyed man raised a finger to silence Dr. Krenik. "Doctor, you can leave now," he said and turned to address Jean. "My name is Agent Smyte. It's my understanding that you took a DNA test today. Is that correct?"

Jean stared at the golden pin on Agent Smyte's tie. It was a scythe.

Suddenly, Agent Smyte grabbed Jean's jaw and squeezed it, forcing her lips to peel apart. "I will not ask you again. Did you take a DNA test?" he said, releasing Jean's jaw from his grip.

Jean trembled with fear, and her heart raced. She coughed and cleared her throat. "Uh, yeah. But it was inconclusive."

Agent Smyte smirked. "Oh, I believe there was more to it than that." He stood and turned toward the men standing behind him. "Okay, let's get out of here."

A burly man picked Jean up and carried her toward the SUV in his arms. Her heart pounded. She wriggled and leaned to the side but could not get away from his tight hold. Suddenly, a loud engine roared and a sleek motorcycle sped toward them. Jean seized her chance to escape. She thrashed in the man's arms, kicking her legs and squirming to loosen his iron grip. "Let go of me," she screamed, driving her elbow into his ribs.

The man grunted in pain, but he did not release her. Jean twisted violently and was able to wrench herself halfway out of his grasp. Before she could completely break free, the man slammed her against the SUV and shoved her inside it.

A motorcycle swerved, nearly colliding with the man who carried Jean. Then, it slid across the gravel before coming to a complete stop. The rider hopped off the motorcycle, turned toward Jean and the men, and removed his helmet. The rider was a man with a lean, muscular build who appeared to be in his early twenties. His hair was a mop of short black curls that framed a chiseled face. His eyes were a light brown, like caramel. His lips were full and curved into a smirk as he walked toward Jean.

Jean banged on the window. "Help!" she yelled. "Please help me!"

The young man from the motorcycle stepped forward. "What's going on?"

Dr. Krenik nodded at the young man, climbed into his car, and drove away.

Agent Smyte walked toward the SUV and motioned to two burly men standing nearby. "Deal with him."

The men strode toward the young man, their heavy boots thudding on the pavement. The young man's muscles tensed as his sharp eyes tracked their advance. As the first man reached for his shoulder with meaty fingers, the young man seized the man's arm in an iron grip, yanking him off balance before delivering a savage punch directly between his eyes. Blood erupted from the man's shattered nose as he crumpled to the ground.

Before the young man could react, a short but solidly built attacker wrapped his thick arms around him from behind, squeezing viciously. The young man grunted as he drove his heel hard into his attacker's groin. Cursing in pain, the attacker released his grip. In one smooth motion, the young man gripped his attacker's arm, squatted, and heaved the burly man over his shoulder, slamming him brutally against the pavement.

Three men rushed toward the young man. He launched into motion, unleashing a barrage of precise blows—a lightning quick jab to the first man's throat, followed by a spinning kick that sent him flying into the wall. He then dropped to the ground, sweeping the next man's legs from under him and striking him with a quick elbow jab. The young man slammed his heel into the third man's stomach, sending him to the ground writhing in pain.

The man who put Jean in the back seat of the SUV turned around and faced the young man, who then hit him with a single punch, knocking him out. Agent Smyte hopped into the other SUV and sped away.

The young man helped Jean out of the vehicle. "Let's get out of here before these goons wake up." He grabbed her hand and hurried her over to his motorcycle. "Here, take this," he said, handing her his helmet.

Jean hesitated before reaching for the helmet. *So, I have two choices. Stay or ... well, he definitely looks like the better option.*

"It's not safe for you here. We need to leave."

As Jean slid the helmet onto her head and climbed onto the back of the motorcycle, a knot formed in her stomach. She swallowed hard, trying to push away the rising wave of fear threatening to consume her.

The young man hopped onto the motorcycle and glanced over his shoulder. "I'm Jamal."

Hopefully, I won't fall. Jean wrapped her arms around Jamal's waist as he revved the bike's engine. "Oh, I'm Jean."

As they peeled away, leaving the mysterious attackers writhing in the gravel, Jean tightened her grip around Jamal's waist. "Thank you," she said breathlessly. She knew nothing about this stranger beyond his name. But something in his confident, steady voice set her nerves at ease.

8

Running from Danger

Jean felt safe with her arms wrapped snuggly around Jamal's waist. As they picked up speed, the wind pummeled her face, so she leaned forward, catching a whiff of Jamal's woodsy cologne mixed with sweat. Suddenly, the motorbike jerked and slid as its front tire rolled over a large pothole. Jean's chest tightened and her breathing became strained. She tapped Jamal on the shoulder. "Pull over."

"Huh?"

"Pull over!" Jean yelled.

As Jamal stepped on the rear brake control, his motorcycle shook. They reached the side of the road and climbed off the motorcycle. The speed of Jean's breathing intensified, and she stumbled sideways, plopping onto the ground as the steady hum of tires rolling on pavement echoed in the background. After steadying herself, Jean sat on her knees and leaned forward before taking several deep belly breaths. *That was scary. I thought for sure I was going to fall. This has to be the worst night of my life. I wish I was at home in bed.*

A worried expression marred Jamal's face. "Oh crap. Are you okay?" he asked as he rubbed his hand through his short, black hair and squatted down next to Jean.

Yeah, now that I'm not on a motorcycle going 100 miles per hour with a stranger who ... Jean glanced at Jamal and tilted her chin. "How'd you do that?"

Jamal scrunched his eyebrows and frowned. "Do what?"

Jean sighed. "You just took down something like twenty men," she exclaimed. *Is he some type of hitman? Or in a gang or the mafia? Should I try to flag down the police?*

Jamal shrugged and shot her a crooked grin. "I guess all those kung-fu lessons my parents forced on me finally paid off."

As she continued taking a series of deep breaths, Jean shut her eyes and curled into a ball.

"Are you sure you're okay?"

"I'll be fine."

"Okay, I'm going to check out my bike. Let me know if you need something." Jamal slid a small flashlight out of his pocket and circled his motorcycle while repeatedly glancing in Jean's direction.

"Damn," Jamal exclaimed.

"What's wrong?" Jean hopped up and strolled over to Jamal.

"The front brake rotor broke. There's no way we'll make it much further on this bike. We'll have to hike it." Jamal moved his bike behind a bushy area off the shoulder. "I'll come back to get it later." He pointed toward a cluster of lights in the distance. "I believe there's an exit with some motels nearby. It's not too far. We can crash for the night."

Jean and Jamal began walking along the highway's shoulder. As they walked, Jean's eyes darted back and forth toward the highway's traffic while Jamal rubbed his hands together. "Ooh, winter is coming. Let's hurry to get out of this cold." He lowered his jacket off his shoulders and held it toward Jean. "Here, take this."

Jean shook her head and scrunched her brows. "You're cold?"

"Of course. I think it's around 30 or 40 degrees. What, you're not cold?"

Jean shrugged. "No, I feel fine." It suddenly dawned on Jean that she never felt cold. Sometimes, a fleeting chill would pass through her veins, but it always dissipated within minutes. "You don't think we should call a taxi or something?"

"We're so close to the exit. We can make it there before a cab gets here. And, it's too cold to stand here. At least I'll warm up by walking," Jamal said as he pulled his jacket back up onto his shoulders. "So, what was going on with you and those men?"

Jean shrugged. "I have no idea," she mumbled, her voice trembling with fear. "The whole thing was really weird." Jean glanced around the empty road. "I think they were trying to kidnap me."

"Well, if we run into them again, I'll take care of them for you."

"I don't doubt that."

They continued to walk until they arrived at a small hotel. "Oh no," Jean said with a worried look on her face.

"What's wrong?"

"I don't have my phone." She slipped her hands into her pockets as if searching for her phone. *Why am I doing that? I never keep my phone in my pocket.* "It must be in my car."

"I have a phone. Also, the hotel has one."

"I know, but I also had a bag with clothes and things." Jean stuck her hands in her pants pockets. "I don't have my money."

"Don't worry. I'll get us a room. You don't mind sharing, do you? I'll get one with two beds. If that's not available, I'll sleep in a chair or something."

"I promise I'll pay you back." Jean secretly wished she could have her own room. After all, Jamal was a stranger. But, she had no money and she was too exhausted to think about anything. He seemed safe enough and he did just save her life.

"No worries. Do you want to borrow my phone?"

"Um, that's okay. I was going to call my mom, but I can wait until we get to the room."

Jamal slid his phone out of his pocket and waved it in front of Jean. "Are you sure? I don't mind if you use it."

Jean hesitated. "Um, okay. Thanks." Jean raised her arm to grab the phone, but Jamal lifted it higher in the air away from her.

"Hey, make sure you return it. If you steal my phone and run away, I know people."

"Even if I run, I'm sure I won't get very far. I mean, with your kung fu skills and all, I'm sure you'll take me down."

Jamal chuckled and handed the phone to Jean. "Oh, by the way, my number shows up as a private call," he said.

"Thanks." Jean stepped away out of earshot of Jamal and dialed her mother's number. The call went straight to voicemail. "Hey, Mom, this is Jean. I just wanted to let you know I stopped at a hotel on my way to Seattle. I borrowed someone else's phone. Anyway, I just wanted to update you. I'll try to reach you again later. Love you."

After checking into a double room, Jamal bought Jean a pair of leggings and a sweatshirt from the hotel's gift shop. Upon entering the room, Jean's hands trembled as she scanned the room with a worried expression. *What have I gotten myself into? Maybe I should have had him drop me off at the hotel and go on his merry way. I'm sure he has a friend or family member nearby who can pick him up.*

Jamal slid past Jean. "Are you okay?"

Um, not really. I'm in a hotel room with a complete stranger. Of course, I'm not okay. "Um, y-yeah. I'm f-fine."

"Are you sure? Maybe I'll get a separate room."

He's already done so much for me. Maybe I can borrow his phone and text his information to my parents. "Um, that's okay. Can I see your ID?"

"Sure." Jamal slid his driver's license out of his pocket and handed it to Jean.

"Thanks. Can I borrow your phone again? I just want to make sure my parents know who I'm with."

"Of course," Jamal said, handing his phone to her.

Jean snapped a picture of the license and sent a text message to her parents with the image. After returning the phone and license, she carried her new clothes into the bathroom and locked the door. *Let me make sure it's really locked.* She jiggled the doorknob several times before showering and changing her clothes. Before leaving the bathroom, she grabbed a towel and wiped away the steam from the bathroom mirror. Jean stared at her reflection, examining her familiar features and searching for signs of alien otherness. But all she saw was the same ordinary human. She blinked a few times. Her eyes appeared to be a more golden orange than their usual brown. *Maybe I'm just tired.* She rubbed her fingers against her face. Her skin shimmered with a warm, golden hue.

Jean continued to study her reflection in the foggy mirror, puzzled by the fleeting changes in her eyes and skin. A whisper in the back of her mind wondered if the DNA test had unlocked something hidden deep within her genome. She sighed, brushed her hand over her arm, and pinched her skin. *Is it true? Can I really be half-alien?* Jean's heart rate soared, so she took a few deep breaths to steady it. *No, it can't be true. I look human. I feel human. Aliens aren't real.*

Jamal tapped on the bathroom door. "Are you okay in there?"

Jean shook her head as she tried to clear her racing thoughts and flung the door open. "Oh, yeah. I'm sorry."

"No worries." Jamal sat down on the small sofa. "Take as much time as you need. I was just worried."

Jean sighed and sat on the edge of the bed farthest from the door. "Jamal, do you believe in aliens?"

"Wait, you didn't see an alien in the bathroom, did you?" Jamal hopped up and peeked into the bathroom.

Jean giggled. "I'm serious. Do you believe aliens exist?"

"Well, there's a lot of space out in outer space. Wouldn't it be a waste if humans were the only ones?"

Jean sighed. "I suppose."

"I mean, I believe in a lot of wacky stuff, so I'm probably not the best person to ask," he said with a slight shrug, his voice tinged with a hint of amusement.

"Oh, that's okay," she replied, her shoulders slumping with disappointment. "Your insight is helpful. Have you ever taken a DNA test?"

"If you're pregnant, it's not mine. You're cute and everything, but we just met, and I barely touched you."

Jean laughed so hard a few tears fell out of her eyes. She wiped her eyes with her sleeve and cleared her throat. "Well, anyway, it's not important. I shouldn't have said anything."

Jamal looked at Jean curiously. "If there's something going on, feel free to tell me. Maybe I can help."

Jean hesitated. *He'll probably think I'm crazy.*

"No pressure. If you don't want to tell me…"

"Okay." Jean took a deep breath and rubbed her palms across her thighs. "Don't laugh, but I think those men were after me because I took a DNA test."

Jamal leaned forward. "Why?"

Jean shrugged. "I don't know, but I think it may have something to do with my biological parents. I never met them because I'm adopted. In fact, I was on my way to meet my biological brother in Seattle. With what happened, it's now more important than ever that I find my biological family." Jamal studied her closely. *Why did I say something? He doesn't believe me. He thinks I'm delusional.*

"If you want, I can go with you. I don't have any plans and I can take care of things if those men show up again."

"You've already done so much. I'm sure I'll be okay."

"I love an adventure. Besides, how else will I get that money you owe me?"

Jean giggled. "Well, I guess it will be fun to travel with a comedian. Are you sure it won't be a problem? Won't your, um, employer have a problem if you skip out on work tomorrow? Or are you a student?"

"It's your lucky day. I just happen to be free tomorrow." Jamal winked at Jean as his mouth curled into a slight grin.

"Well, I don't want to be held responsible if you lose your job. What do you do for a living, anyway?"

"I could tell you, but then I'd have to kill you."

Jean rolled her eyes. "You couldn't come up with anything more original than that?"

"Look, I do undercover work. I can't provide details."

Jean's eyes widened as she cocked her head. "You're a police officer?" She imagined him walking around a police station wearing a blue uniform with a gun at his hip.

"I may have already said too much. You've had a long day. Let's talk after you get some rest." Jamal's phone rang, and he glanced at it. "Excuse me, I need to take this call." He left the room and closed the door.

Jean hopped up and pressed her ear against the door. She overheard Jamal say everything was okay, and she was safe. *Who is he talking to? Did he tell someone about me?* A few minutes later, the doorknob rattled and Jean sprinted to the bed on her toes, slid under the covers, and squeezed her eyes shut just as Jamal opened the door. She lay still, struggling to slow her racing thoughts.

A few minutes later, Jamal's phone buzzed. Peeking through barely parted lids, Jean saw Jamal frown down at his phone. His jaw clenched tight as he read a text message. With a tense glance at a seemingly sleeping Jean, he deleted it and shoved the phone in his pocket. Jamal stared at the ceiling with a hard glint in his eyes.

Jean closed her eyes. *He seemed bothered by that message. What's going on? Who is he communicating with?* Her weary mind spun, eroding her brief sense of security. She had wanted to believe Jamal was simply a good Samaritan who saved her by chance. But now, unease gripped her. Whatever they were facing, this was only the beginning. The danger was still out there and she didn't know if her supposed protector was being completely honest.

9

Missing Person

Emmie and Carmen lay in their cozy beds, lost in deep slumber, when suddenly, Emmie's phone alarm blared, slicing through the peaceful silence of the room. With a groggy haze enveloping her mind, Emmie picked up the buzzing phone parked next to her in bed, letting out a soft groan. After she pried her heavy eyelids open, she squinted at the screen, the soft glow illuminating her sleepy face.

Carmen rolled onto her side, rubbing her eyes. "What time is it?" she questioned, her voice still laced with drowsiness.

Emmie released a boisterous yawn. "Uh, six-thirty," she grumbled, her voice quavering as she descended the ladder of her loft bed. Her arms shook with fatigue as she lowered each foot, searching blindly in the dark for the next rung.

Carmen's squinted gaze wandered over to Jean's empty bed. "Jean's out already?"

Emmie nodded, her memory slowly awakening. "Remember? She went to meet her brother."

"Oh, right," Carmen muttered. "I wonder if she made it there yet. Did you check the tracker?"

"I'll check it now." Emmie opened the tracker and searched for Jean's location. "Hmm, that's strange."

"What?"

"Her location ain't updated in hours," Emmie muttered, confusion clouding her features as she sat at her desk, staring at her phone.

Carmen slowly climbed down her ladder and leaned over Emmie's shoulder, rubbing her eyes. "That's so weird. It's totally frozen." She reached over Emmie's head and tapped the screen, but the tracking icon stubbornly remained still on the map. "Is it not working?"

"I don't know..." Emmie frowned. "I never had issues before. Look, the time stamp keeps glitchin'. See." She held the phone up to Carmen's face. The erratic timer jumped sporadically before the app abruptly crashed. Emmie rebooted her phone. For a split second, the screen flashed: Tracking Terminated. She gasped as her eyes widened. "Did it delete?"

"Let me see." Carmen yanked the phone out of Emmie's hand. "What did you do? Did you press delete?"

"I didn't do nothin'. I just restarted it."

Carmen released a deep sigh. "You must've done something. Now I can't even find the app." She tapped on the phone's screen, the sound echoing softly. Minutes passed as she searched through the applications and files, her brows furrowing. "Something's not right. I just tried to pull the backup file, but it's corrupted. Good news, we know her last location before it stopped working. Bad news, it was the middle of the highway."

"Well, that's where we'll go then. It's not far. We should drive there just to make sure there isn't a problem. We'll be able to make it back before class if nothin's there."

Carmen let out an exasperated sigh, her eyes rolling in disbelief. "So, let me get this straight. We're just supposed to drive to the middle of the highway and park? I don't think so."

"We'll drive to the area and return if nothin's there. I know which exit sign it was near. It's not that far. Of course, you'll need to drive 'cause I don't trust my hooptie on highways." Emmie poked out her bottom lip. "Please, Carmen," she whined. "This may be a matter of Jean's life or death."

"Why don't we call the police?" Carmen asked, her voice tinged with concern.

"Let's just make this one quick drive," she replied hastily, the urgency clear in her voice. "Then we'll go to the police."

Carmen strolled over to her closet and rummaged through her clothes. "Well, let me shower and get dressed."

"Just throw on some clothes. You can shower when we get back."

"Are you crazy?" Carmen exclaimed, her voice rising in disbelief. "You expect me to go out looking like this?" she asked with her arms outstretched as she turned around in a circle.

As Carmen drove toward the interstate, her knuckles turned white as she gripped the steering wheel. Her eyes darted anxiously, searching for any sign of Jean's car.

"I don't want to scare you, but is there a chance..." Carmen's voice trailed off, her words swallowed by the weight of uncertainty. She took a deep breath, the air heavy with anticipation, before continuing, "Jean's dependable. She wouldn't forget to call us like she promised. If she didn't make it..."

Emmie directed her eyes to her phone and then back up at Carmen. "Don't be so negative. I'm sure she's fine. Maybe she's in an area with a poor connection or her phone died. Let's clear our minds and talk about somethin' else."

"I've been thinking about something. Don't take this the wrong way, but I'm not sure how I feel about having a roommate who's an alien."

Emmie's eyes widened as she gasped. "Carmen, she's our friend! Nothin's changed, and she's human, too." She didn't know what to think about what Carmen had said. Did she feel the same way about other people who were different? Of course, being part alien was a unique type of different, but still...

"Like I said, don't take it the wrong way," Carmen said, pursing her lips. "Anyway, do you think there's a chance she went to her home planet?"

Emmie rolled her eyes. "Ya mean Earth? Her home planet is Earth!"

They drove on, a cloud of tension hanging in the air as they continued in silence. Scenery blurred past them, a mix of industrial buildings and vast expanses of open fields. The sound of their tires on the pavement provided a steady rhythm, punctuated by the occasional honk of a passing car.

After what felt like an eternity, they arrived at the designated area that pinged Jean's location. The surroundings were a blur of concrete and asphalt, the air heavy with the scent of exhaust. Emmie's heart raced as they pulled to a stop, their destination looming before them. Her eyes widened as she pointed at a large tow truck with flashing lights parked on the shoulder. "Wait, is that her car on the truck?"

"It looks like it, but I don't see Jean." Carmen pulled over and parked in front of the truck. "Wow, her car was totaled."

Carmen and Emmie approached the truck. The tow truck driver was busy securing Jean's car to the truck. He had a gruff face with a salt and pepper beard and he donned a gray flannel shirt and loose-fitting, grease-stained jeans that barely hid his beer belly. Emmie tried to get the driver's attention by waving her arms.

"He doesn't see you." Carmen jogged toward the driver, yelling. "Excuse me. This is our friend's car. Where is she?"

"I don't know nothin' about yo' friend," the driver said without looking up.

Carmen inched closer to Jean's car. "Was she taken to the hospital? Did an ambulance

come?"

"Look lady, the only thing that was here when I got here was that piece of a car."

As the driver turned to leave, Emmie rushed forward, blocking his path. "Please, can you tell us somethin'? Anything at all? Was there another car involved in the accident or did you see someone pick up a girl?"

"There were no signs of another damaged vehicle. But..." The words died on his tongue as his eyes narrowed.

"What?" Emmie's body tensed as nervous energy flowed through her veins. "You noticed somethin'?"

The driver glanced suspiciously around before answering in a low tone. "Might've been nothing, but I did see a dark Hummer parked on the shoulder by the vehicle. Tinted windows. Soon as I pulled up, it sped away." The driver started walking toward his truck.

"Wait!" Emmie dashed toward the driver, flailing her arms. "Did someone named Jean order the tow?"

"I only receive pick up location and vehicle description from the service center. Now, if you ladies will excuse me, I'm on the clock," he said, continuing toward his truck.

Emmie stepped forward and lunged between the driver and his truck. "I'm sorry to take up ya time, but can you tell us somethin'? Perhaps, what might have happened?"

"Look, lady, I don't know what happened. It's pretty obvious this car flipped over after being rear-ended. Now, you might wanna call the hospital about your friend." With savage force, the tow truck driver shoved past Emmie, causing her to stumble backward and slip, falling onto the gravel road. Then he climbed into his truck and merged onto the highway as he drove away.

As Emmie sat on the ground trying to regain her composure, Carmen grabbed her hand and helped her to stand. They watched the tow truck as it drove away. For a few moments, they were silent.

Carmen sighed heavily. "Should we call the police first?"

Emmie shook her head no. "I agree with that a-hole. I think we should call hospitals. If she's not in a hospital, then we should file a missing person's report."

"Hey, check the app. Does the tracker show movement?"

Emmie glanced at her phone. A subtle movement of Jean's vehicle traveled along the map. "Yeah, it's moving now. Her phone must be in her car."

Carmen and Emmie raced to call every hospital within a 50-mile radius, their hearts pounding with anxiety. They had to find Jean, and fast. As they called each hospital, they received the same response: no Jean Anderson. Their worst fears were becoming a reality—Jean was missing, and they didn't know where she could be.

Emmie's heart sank. "What do we do now?"

Carmen took a deep breath. "We file a missing person's report. I knew we should have stopped her from going."

A wave of disappointment washed over Emmie. She had thought it was great that Jean was going to learn more about herself by meeting her biological family. Perhaps she should have tried harder to encourage her to wait. Or perhaps she should have gone with her. She would have missed a few classes, but maybe she could have helped with whatever happened. Two people are stronger than one. "I don't think we could have done anything. She was determined. Besides, we didn't know this would happen."

As they drove to the nearest police station, Emmie couldn't help but wonder what could have happened to Jean. The thought of her dear friend hurt or lost somewhere was almost too much to bear. "Do you have her parents' number?"

"No."

"I'll search for it online and try to reach them. Maybe they know somethin'." Emmie entered Jean's name into her phone and found her parents' contact information. She dialed the number for Mrs. Anderson. There was no answer, and the voicemail picked up. "Hello, Mrs. Anderson. This is Jean's roommate, Emmie. I was wondering if you've spoken to Jean. We haven't been able to reach her and we're worried. You can call me at the number on the caller ID or send a text." Emmie ended the call and turned toward Carmen. "That didn't sound crazy, did it?"

"No, it was fine."

As they entered, the police station's stale air and harsh lights made hope feel fragile, but Emmie clung to it with every fiber of her being as she followed the stern officer to his desk. His face remained stone-like as he typed Jean's name and description into the computer.

Beside Emmie, Carmen's neatly manicured nails dug into her palms. "It's been over twelve hours since she left," she exclaimed, raw panic creeping in.

Emmie slid her own clammy hand over Carmen's, stopping its trembling. Carmen responded with a firm squeeze, conveying her wordless thanks.

As they walked out of the police station, Carmen whipped around to face Emmie, eyes flashing. "This is all your fault!" she exclaimed, jabbing a finger at Emmie's chest. "If you hadn't encouraged Jean to go meet those ... those aliens, she would be safe at school right now!"

Emmie recoiled. "That ain't fair! How was I supposed to know somethin' bad would happen?"

Carmen threw her hands up in exasperation. "It was a terrible idea from the start! Didn't you think about why Jean was abandoned as a baby? Maybe her mother was scared of her or maybe her alien relatives were dangerous! And now they've probably abducted her, or worse!"

"You're lettin' your imagination run wild," Emmie retorted, hands curling into fists. "It was probably just a car accident."

"Just a car accident? Then where is she? And why did that truck driver see someone speed off in a tinted SUV?" she shrieked. "Face it—Jean searching for those aliens led to her disappearance!"

Emmie stepped forward, eyes burning with fury. "The only thing I need to face is findin' my friend!" she shouted. "And standin' here pointin' fingers ain't helping!"

She whirled on her heels, stalking away toward Carmen's car as tears pricked her eyes. Why was she attacking her when Jean needed them most? They had to stick together, not tear each other apart. Emmie could only pray their splintering friendship could hold long enough to bring Jean home safely. She had to believe they would find Jean, navigating safely back from whatever unknown darkness had swallowed her. Until Jean returned, she refused to entertain alternatives.

10

Building Relationships

The following morning, Jamal ordered a rental car to drive to Kale's Infinity Art tattoo parlor in Seattle. Waiting for it to be delivered, Jean sat on a bench in front of the hotel, swinging her legs back and forth while Jamal stood nearby, watching for the car. She focused her eyes on the pavement as she thought about the prior day. *How did he happen to show up when someone was trying to kidnap me? That was a strange coincidence. Maybe I should get a ride back to campus. I can borrow money to get home and pay it back through a funds transfer app or mail it to him. Wait, why did he have a Georgia license?*

Jean glanced up and tugged on Jamal's jacket. "Hey, Jamal, can I ask you something?"

"Of course. What's up?" Jamal sat on the bench next to Jean.

"Don't you think it would be better for me to go home? I'm sure you have plenty of things to do with your job, and I'm sure you can't wait to get back home to Georgia."

"Georgia?"

"Well, yeah. Your license said your home was in Georgia."

"Right. These days I'm more of a nomad. It's been two years since I've been there. I travel around the country for work."

Jean raised a brow. "And that work is what?"

Jamal gestured toward the road and smiled. "Our ride's here. Ready to meet your brother?"

"Um, I suppose," Jean sighed as her mind wandered. *I'm not sure if I should go. What if he rejects me? Will he think I'm weird for showing up at his shop? I wonder if he knows about me. What if he's been looking for me his entire life? He might be happy to see me. Anyway, I guess there's no turning back now. I need to focus on the positives. He might have information about my birth family. Maybe he can introduce me to them. Yeah, I need to go.*

When they arrived at the destination several hours later, Jean peeked out the window and hesitated before exiting the car. A vague unease needled the back of her mind. She gazed at the people passing by, suddenly struck by how different she felt from them. Since learning about her Xeno DNA, it was as if an invisible barrier separated her from the rest of humanity. They went about their lives oblivious to aliens in their midst while she now questioned her own identity and place in the world.

Jamal grinned. "You ready? We can always turn around."

"I didn't come this far for nothing." Jean pushed the door open and climbed out of the cab. Her heart raced as she walked toward the tattoo parlor. When she reached the door, she inhaled deeply. She frowned as a man with geometric facial tattoos strode past. The markings seemed almost ... alien. Could they be some kind of Xeno code or symbols? An indicator of secret alliances unknown to ordinary society? The thought sent a shiver down Jean's spine. How deep did this hidden world extend?

Jamal reached around Jean and pushed open the heavy glass door. Upon entering the tattoo parlor, Jean looked around the shop. Fumes resembling bleach mixed with burned rubber assaulted her nostrils. There was a large abstract mural on a side wall and a small reception desk near the entrance. Hard rock music played over speakers barely covering the humming engines of tattoo guns.

Jean walked up to the reception desk and began flipping through a tattoo catalog on the counter. A large partition separated the reception desk from the back of the shop. A few minutes later, a young woman covered in tattoos came from the back.

"Can I help you?"

Jean folded her arms as her breath stalled. "Um, yeah. Uh, Kale Daniels. Is he here?"

"Oh, you wanna see Kale?" The young woman turned and disappeared to the back of the shop. "Hey, Kale," she shouted. "Someone's here to see you."

Several minutes later, a slender man in his late twenties appeared from behind the partition. His dark brown hair was styled in a mid-fade and colorful tattoos peeked above the collar of his T-shirt and decorated his arms. "Hi, I'm Kale. How can I help you?"

Jean stared at him as every muscle in her body froze. *It's him. I think I can see a slight family resemblance. We have the same nose and face shape. What should I say?*

"Can we go somewhere private?" Jamal asked.

Kale hesitated and looked at Jean. "Uh, sure." He led them to a small, cluttered office at the back of the shop. "Have a seat. What's this about?"

Jean almost tripped over a box on the floor as she sat down in the chair in front of Kale's desk. She inhaled deeply. "Do you remember taking a DNA test?"

Kale scrunched his thick eyebrows. "Yeah."

Jean turned toward Jamal. "Well. Um…"

Jamal stood up. "I'm gonna leave you two alone. Jean, I'll wait for you outside." Jamal left the office.

Jean rubbed her hands on her pants, smoothing them. "Well, um, I think you're my brother."

Kale leaned back in his chair. "How's that?"

"Well, I took the DNA test yesterday, and you showed up as my half-brother. Did you see that?"

Kale clenched his fists, knuckles cracking under the pressure. "No, I didn't see it."

"Oh." Jean's heart sank, her face growing hot with embarrassment. She lowered her eyes toward the floor, wiping her clammy palms on her jeans. *Crap, I should have listened to my roommates. He must think I'm some type of obsessive stalker.*

"I'm sorry. I thought my settings didn't allow others to see my information."

Jean stood. "I'm sorry. I can leave. I didn't mean to…"

"No, that's okay. Stay." Kale leaned forward, resting his elbows on his desk. "So, tell me about yourself, Sis."

Jean raised her eyes and relaxed. *Good. He's okay with me being here.* "Well, I just started college a few months ago. My last foster parents adopted me after I spent years in the system. And now I'm just trying to learn more about my family history. I don't know anything about my bio parents because I was found abandoned at a park. What about you?"

"Hmm, I'm a tattoo artist. I've owned this shop for seven years. I have a couple of guys working for me."

"What about your childhood? Um, do you know Azon? He's listed as my father."

Kale glared at Jean without blinking. "Well, I spent my entire childhood in foster care. I was never adopted. My mom passed away soon after childbirth and I ended up in the system."

"So, we were both foster kids. Do you know Azon?"

"When I turned eighteen, I applied to join the army. They required me to take a DNA test. That was nine years ago. The army was my dream—the only place I ever imagined belonging," Kale muttered, scowling. "It was ripped away because of DNA from Azon."

Jean bristled. "You don't know Azon's the reason. Our DNA came from both parents."

Kale slammed his palm on his desk. "The undetermined part came from him! If his freak genes hadn't mixed in with my mother's, I would've been cleared."

Heat flooded Jean's cheeks at the venom in Kale's words. "Don't call it freak DNA! He's our father. He's a part of us."

"Some father," Kale bellowed. "He abandoned us! But his rotten DNA stuck around just long enough to ruin everything."

Jean's eyebrows shot to her hairline as she fought to steady her frustration. "It's unfair to blame Azon for choices outside his control. We don't know his full story."

With every word, Kale's face grew more red. "His story? I know all I need to know."

Jean let out a deep sigh. "Did they say specifically why they rejected you? Did they say it was from your DNA test results?"

Kale shrugged. "No. I never got an answer, but half of my ethnicity came back as undetermined."

"Mine was undetermined too. Well, 62% was undetermined."

Kale sat silent for a moment. "62%? That's strange. We only inherit 50% from each parent. How do you have 62% of undetermined DNA?"

"I don't know. This is all new to me. The test confirmed we share the same father." Jean leaned forward and rested her head on her palm. "Hmm. I'm not that much closer to getting information about my parents than I was before the test. Do you know anything about our father?"

Kale sighed. "Uh, not really," he mumbled. "The only thing I know is that my mother went to a fertility clinic owned by a well-known doctor—a Dr. Gravin. I saw his name in my birth records. I'm sorry I can't be of any help."

"Do you think that doctor might have information about our father?"

"I doubt it." Kale shifted forward in his seat and started fiddling with a pen between his fingers. "I never thought about that. I'm not sure why he would have information about him. I'm sure he had information about my mother since she was his patient." He leaned back in his chair, almost tipping it over.

"I wonder if my mother might be connected to him also."

"How?"

Jean shrugged. "I'm not sure, but it might be worth investigating. I mean, maybe our father was a sperm donor at the clinic or something like that."

Kale remained silent with a blank expression. He focused his gaze on the door as if he was trying to figure out a reason to leave.

"Kale, can I ask you something?"

"What?" Kale asked, directing his glance toward Jean.

"Okay, this may be a strange question, but..." Jean straightened her posture. "Does your body have any unique anomalies? For example, sometimes other people say they're cold, but I never feel that way."

Kale stared blankly at Jean. "Everyone has a different reaction to temperature."

"Let me back up for a second. After I got my results, I did some research. DNA stands for deoxyribonucleic acid. It's a molecule that contains genetic information encoding all traits passed from parents to offspring." She drew a spiral DNA symbol in the air with her finger. "DNA is made up of pairing nucleotide bases—adenine, thymine, cytosine, and guanine. The order of these base pairs makes up genes that determine eye color, height, disease risk, and so on. It's like nature's blueprint. When your DNA was flagged, it likely means those base chemicals had sections that didn't match normal, expected human genes." Curling her lips downward, Jean sighed. "I know everyone reacts to temperature differently, but I also seem different in hot weather. Even when it's 100 degrees, I don't feel hot. There has to be something in my DNA causing that reaction."

Kale's piercing eyes narrowed in thought. "Well, I don't know about hot or cold temperatures, but I have great eyesight that's above average. It really helps with my tattoo business, and it's the main reason I thought I'd make a good army sniper."

Jean raised a brow and gave Kale a curious stare. "Hmm. I think I would like to pay that Dr. Gravin a visit."

Kale scrunched his brows. "Really? Why?"

"He might have information about my mother and our father. Maybe we can find out what's wrong with our DNA."

"I want nothing to do with Azon," Kale huffed. "It was his fault that my DNA was not good enough for the army. And if he really cared about me, why didn't he come get me so I didn't have to stay in foster care?"

"How do you know it was his fault? You inherited DNA from both parents."

Stretching his arms forward, Kale cracked his knuckles. "I know which DNA came from him."

"Oh," Jean looked at the floor and sighed. "I don't know. I just feel so lost. It's hard to explain." Leaning forward, Jean rested her head in her palm as she glanced at Kale and struggled to hold back tears fighting to be released from her eyes. Although she longed to learn more about her Xeno heritage, doubts plagued her. Was embracing these newfound roots a betrayal of the loving parents who raised her? Did she even belong in the human world anymore? But when she imagined never discovering that missing piece of her identity, her heart ached. She struggled to find her place, torn between two worlds.

Kale was silent for a moment, shifting in his seat. He made eye contact with Jean, and his expression softened. "Okay, maybe I can help," he said as he stood. "Let me see if I can clear my schedule and make a couple of phone calls. I can't make any promises, but I might be able to take you to see Dr. Gravin."

Jean's eyes perked up. "Really?"

Kale strolled toward the door. Yeah. I guess I hate seeing my sister in so much despair. But are you absolutely sure?"

"About what?"

"Are you sure you want to do this? You never know what can of worms you'll open. Some things are better left alone."

"I understand what you're saying, but I just want answers. If my bio parents end up being terrible people, I'll just go back to my life. But at least I'll have answers and know where my DNA came from."

"Hmm, I get it," Kale said as he reached for the doorknob. "I remember being like you once. Young, naïve, without a care in the world." Kale slid his phone out of his pocket and left the room.

Jean frowned. Kale's words stung. Sure, she was young. But she never thought of herself as being naïve. Okay, maybe it was naïve to hop up and drive to see an unknown brother in an unfamiliar location. And maybe it was naïve to trust someone you just met and share a hotel room with him. But you can accomplish nothing without taking risks, right?

After a half hour, Kale returned. "Okay, I couldn't reach my next client to cancel. I'll do his tattoo and then I have to clean up the shop before I leave. It will be kinda late when I'm done, so it might be best to head out to the doctor's office tomorrow morning."

11

Unanswered Calls

After returning home from the doctor, the Andersons headed to the living room. Shadows stretched across the plush brown carpet and consumed the room's corners. Mrs. Anderson switched on a lamp, casting a warm glow on the photos lining the aged walls. She focused on Jean's fifth grade school photo, wishing she could reach through time and protect that innocent girl from the world.

Mrs. Anderson pulled her phone out of her purse and tapped on the screen. "That's strange. I have a missed call from a private number."

"Did they leave a voicemail?"

"I can't get into my voicemail. And it looks like there's a text message, but it's not downloading. You'd think with all this newfangled technology, they'd be able to make something that would work right half the time. Jean was supposed to call, and I haven't heard from her. I hope nothing's wrong." Mrs. Anderson's hands trembled as she tapped her daughter's name on the phone's glowing screen. Putting the phone to her ear, she listened to the sound of Jean's voicemail message. "Hey Jean. I'm calling to make sure you're okay. Call or text me. Love you."

Mrs. Anderson sighed. "Something's not right. Her phone went straight to voicemail. I'm really worried." Mrs. Anderson repeatedly dialed Jean's number. Voicemail again. "Jean, honey, this is your mom again. Please call me as soon as you can."

"She hasn't been gone that long. Try to relax. I'm sure she just has her phone off," Mr. Anderson said, looking up from his tablet over his reading glasses. "Our girl's probably just distracted by catching up with her brother," Mr. Anderson offered calmly. "Let's not assume the worst."

"I can't relax. Four calls and still no answer? That's not like her. Even when she's in class, she sends a quick call back later message." Mrs. Anderson sat stiffly on the edge of the sofa and massaged the tension strangling the back of her neck.

"Let's give her 30 more minutes. If we don't hear from her, I'll pull up her roommates' numbers from the directory. We'll see if they heard from her." Mr. Anderson pressed his tablet off and walked toward the kitchen. "I'm concerned too, but working ourselves up into a panic won't help."

Mrs. Anderson's thumb hesitated over her daughter's name. *What if Jean lay injured somewhere, unable to answer her phone? Or what if she'd been assaulted after stopping at a gas station, like that girl on the news last month?* Her stomach twisted into a thousand knots. "Let's go to Seattle. I'm sure she won't mind. We can meet her brother and treat them to dinner."

Mr. Anderson let out a deep sigh. "Honey, I don't feel up to driving to Seattle, especially after all that bloodwork."

The sofa's coarse floral fabric prickled Mrs. Anderson's arms as she hunched over the too-bright screen of her phone, wishing it would ring and light up with Jean's name. The ticking of the oak grandfather clock in the hall seemed to grow louder as she strained her ears for a ringtone that never came.

DING DONG! DING DONG!

Mr. Anderson strolled from the kitchen carrying a glass of orange juice. "Are you expecting a package?"

"No."

Mr. Anderson hurried to view the security feed, his pulse increasing at the sight of two men and one woman at the door. All three were wearing military fatigues and had serious facial expressions. "Can I help you?" Mr. Anderson asked shakily into the microphone.

A man's deep voice came through the speaker. "Yes, we need to talk to you about your daughter, Jean."

12

Lost and Found

After leaving the police station, Carmen and Emmie headed back to campus. Upon arriving on campus, they parked the car and marched to their dorm. Emmie peeked over her shoulder. Someone seemed to follow them. She edged closer to Carmen and whispered. "I think that girl is following us."

Carmen whipped her head around. "What girl?"

"Shh ... don't look." Emmie picked up her pace.

"It's probably just a coincidence. There are a lot of students on campus and some of them live in our dorm. Also, it's not like there aren't other dorms next to our building."

Emmie sighed. "I guess you're right." As she walked, Emmie couldn't shake the feeling that they were being followed. She quickly peeked over her shoulder and saw a petite girl with a university hoodie pulled snugly around her head.

When they arrived at the dorm, Emmie scanned her ID to unlock the door and entered, with Carmen following closely behind. When the door was almost closed, the girl following them grabbed the handle and entered the building. Emmie and Carmen rode the elevator to their floor and walked to their room.

"See, I told you we weren't being followed," Carmen said as she sat at her desk and sighed. "I can't believe I missed two classes today."

"Yeah, but I can't think about classes now. I'm gonna make some flyers with Jean's picture and post them around campus if we don't hear from her before tomorrow."

"Okay, and I'll meet with the resident advisor to let her know what's going on. I'll ask her to put letters in everyone's mailbox asking anyone with information to contact us or the police."

"I'm surprised you wanna do somethin' to help find the alien," Emmie said sarcastically.

Carmen slumped her shoulders. "Look, I need to apologize for what I said about Jean earlier. I really didn't mean anything. I just ... I guess I felt scared realizing aliens actually exist. I mean, I've heard stories about alien abductions and UFO sightings, but it was still strange learning Jean might be part alien. I like Jean. She's a good friend and if she's part alien, I can accept that."

Emmie's lips curled into a smile. "Apology accepted."

A few minutes later, someone knocked on the door. Emmie opened it to find the girl with the hoodie standing there. Blonde strands of hair peeked out from the front of the hoodie. Emmie's eyes widened. "Oh, can I help you?"

"Hi, is Jean here?"

Emmie and Carmen glanced at each other. Carmen hopped off her bed and walked over to the door.

"She's not here. Can we help you?" Carmen asked.

The girl shifted her weight, slowly rocking from side to side. "Oh no, I really need to speak with Jean. Do you know when she'll be back?"

"We actually don't know where she is or when she'll be back." Carmen's face scrunched up in worry. "Have you seen her today?"

"No, I don't think so. I never met her before, but I need to tell her something. It's really important."

Emmie grabbed a small notebook off her desk. "I can take a message and pass it along to her when she comes back."

"No, that's okay. I should go." The girl turned away from Emmie and Carmen.

"Do you wanna leave your number?" Emmie asked.

"No." The girl glanced at her cellphone. "I should ... I have to go." The girl spun around and scurried down the hallway toward the elevator.

Emmie slammed the door. "That was weird."

"Yeah, what do you think she wanted?"

Emmie peeked out the door. "I don't know. Maybe we should follow her."

Carmen shot Emmie an incredulous look. "You want to stalk her?"

"It's just strange that she suddenly came here after Jean disappeared. We never saw her before and she refused to provide information," Emmie huffed. "You don't have to go with me, but I'm going."

"Okay, but let's keep our distance because we don't want her to see us. We need to hurry before we lose her."

Emmie and Carmen rushed downstairs and darted out of the dorm. The sun was beginning to set, casting a warm glow across campus. Emmie squinted as she scanned the walkways, searching for a petite figure in a school hoodie. The campus was abuzz with students milling around or walking in various directions. Many of them wore university hoodies and sweatshirts.

"I guess we lost her," Carmen said, leaning forward with her hands on her thighs as she wheezed.

"Let's keep looking." Emmie headed toward the Student Union, with Carmen following closely behind when she saw a girl wearing a school hoodie entering the building. "I think that's her," Emmie said, pointing.

Emmie and Carmen sprinted toward the girl. When they reached her, Emmie tapped on the girl's shoulder. "Excuse me."

The girl swung around, and the hoodie slipped off her head revealing long, black hair. "Yes?"

Emmie gasped. "Oh, I'm sorry. I thought you were someone else."

The girl smiled. "No worries."

"Maybe we should go back. It's too late. I don't think we'll find her," Carmen said.

Emmie rotated around, scanning the crowd of students when she saw another girl in a school hoodie ducking around a corner near the science building. Emmie tugged at Carmen's arm and pointed in that direction. "Over there! She just went around that building," she said.

"Are you sure?"

"Yeah, I caught a glimpse of her face. Hurry, let's go!" Emmie dashed toward the building, determined not to lose her.

13

Following Clues

Emmie's gaze stayed glued to the back of the girl's hoodie as she led them farther and farther from the bustling campus center.

"We're going to get caught," Carmen muttered.

Up ahead, the girl paused at a crosswalk. Emmie quickly steered Carmen behind a telephone pole, heart pounding. The girl strode toward a small, brown, two-story building with one-way glass windows on the outskirts of campus. With a swift glance over her shoulder, the woman slipped through the unmarked entrance and disappeared.

Emmie tugged Carmen across the street toward the ominous building. Upon arriving at the building's entrance, Emmie's brow creased with worry. "Should we just wait here until she comes out?"

Carmen shrugged. "Maybe. How long do you think we should wait?"

"I don't know. I really don't want to just stand here all day." Squaring her shoulders, Emmie tugged on the door, but it didn't open. "Ugh, I guess we have no choice but to wait."

"Yeah, but I refuse to wait here all day. Anyway, this whole thing is weird. I really don't think…"

The door to the building swung open, and a woman with a wide smile stepped forward. "I'm sorry about that. Chuck is usually here to greet applicants, but he had to step away for a moment. I hope you weren't waiting long."

"Um, no," Emmie said.

"Great," the woman said, gesturing toward the entrance. "Come in. My name is Aris."

As Emmie and Carmen entered the building, the sleek metal walls and glowing blue screens looked high-tech compared to the nondescript exterior. Strange symbols and diagrams dotted some screens. A small robot whirred past them, carrying a tray of medical vials, nearly causing Carmen to leap back in fright.

Carmen leaned close to Emmie's ear, whispering. "This is way more than just some student group. What is this place?"

Emmie shrugged. *If this girl doesn't hush, she's gonna get us in trouble. How am I supposed to know what this place is? I ain't been here before.*

Aris led Emmie and Carmen toward down a long hallway until they reached a rectangular table with a stack of clipboards holding white pieces of paper. Upon reaching the table, she picked up tablets. "Who referred you?"

Carmen stood motionless with her mouth gaping open.

"Um, Jean Anderson," Emmie muttered.

Aris scrunched her brows. "Who?"

"Jean Anderson," Emmie said.

Aris perused the tablet, tapping it with a slim stylus for a few minutes. "Okay, enter your full names and contact information," she said, handing the tablet to Emmie.

Gripping the glowing tablet tight, Emmie typed her name on the signup sheet, hungry to discover the truth. A nervous exhilaration flooded her veins. If this mysterious group had some connection to Jean and her Xeno DNA results, Emmie surmised the secrets they uncovered might prove even wilder than she imagined. Carmen stood motionless with her mouth gaping open.

After Emmie and Carmen entered their information, Aris took the tablet back, scanning their information with pursed lips. "Jean Anderson, you said?" Her eyes narrowed.

Emmie's mouth went dry. "Y-yes, our roommate."

Fingers flying across the screen, Aris asked in a too-sweet voice, "And she referred you personally? Recently?"

"Um, well, not exactly b—" Emmie froze as the woman held up one long finger.

"Let me just ... confirm something. One moment." With a thin smile that didn't reach her eyes, Aris stepped away, heels clicking down the hall.

Carmen gripped Emmie's arm, her face growing leached of any color. "Oh no, we shouldn't have come. What if they call the police?" she whispered harshly.

Emmie shook her head, swooping nervousness twisting in her gut. "Don't worry. We'll just say it was a mix-up if anything happens."

Carmen's eyes widened as if they were going to pop out of her head. "Mix-up? A mix-up? So what, there was a mix-up and we followed the wrong person? Or was the mix-up that we gave the wrong referral name? Please enlighten me."

As the minutes passed without Aris' return, Emmie's forehead creased with concern. *What will we do if security comes? It's my fault. I got us into this mess. Maybe we should just leave.*

Before Emmie could reply, Aris reappeared through an automatic sliding door wearing a bright, toothy grin. "So sorry, just had to double check your referral's status. All set now! Let me take you to our orientation room..." Pressing her hand against a panel, the wall shifted open, revealing a cavernous room. Sharp tingles spread over Emmie's skin as they entered. The conference room contained a long, glowing table with a flickering holographic display at its center.

Emmie released a huge breath of relief.

Aris handed them a clipboard with an application attached. "Find a seat. When you're done with the application, add your name to the list on the front table. We interview one at a time in the order of names on the list. We don't accept everyone for the program, but you can always apply next year. Good luck." Aris left the room.

A short table with snacks sat at the back of the room, and there were several short square tables arranged in a rectangle. Carmen and Emmie sat at one table and began filling out the application form.

Carmen whispered to Emmie, "What are we applying for?"

Emmie shrugged. "Doesn't matter. If they give you an offer, you don't have to take it."

Carmen giggled. "In that case, I might as well have fun with it. Let's see, favorite hobbies. Hmm ... I guess that would be going to parties."

A tall man with broad shoulders walked to the front of the room. He cleared his throat and spoke into the microphone on the podium. "Good morning, everyone. Thank you for coming out here today. My name is Mr. Johnson, and I'm one of three interviewers for the program. Before we begin, let me explain the selection process. Our organization is highly exclusive, and it's important that we recruit a variety of people with unique skills. We're especially looking for individuals with strong physical and mental capabilities, as well as exceptional problem-solving skills. If you have a special talent that fits a need within our organization, we are more likely to select you. After the interview, we will complete full background checks. If we select you for the next phase, you will be required to submit to physical and psychological exams next week. Please note, there is a confidentiality agreement at the end of your application. You must read and sign the agreement before your interview."

A young man raised his hand. Mr. Johnson nodded. "What's the expected time commitment?" the young man asked.

"During the first 8 weeks in the program, you will be required to attend training sessions every weekend. Then you will be assigned to a cohort based on your skills and interests. The cohorts may have additional training requirements."

Carmen leaned over to Emmie. "Sounds like boot camp to me," she whispered.

Emmie giggled. "What do you know about boot camp?"

Mr. Johnson cleared his throat and continued. "After you complete training, you can pick your schedule based on your availability. As this is a volunteer organization, there is no minimum time requirement. The program is not for everyone and you can quit at any time. Many of our volunteers enjoy the experience and become employees of our parent company after graduation. Now, all of you are here only because a friend or family member referred you to our organization."

Carmen scrunched her face and mouthed the word, "Oops."

"I trust each and every one of you to maintain the secrecy upon which we built this organization, whether or not you are selected as a member. The interviews will begin in a few minutes."

Carmen scooted her chair back. "We should leave," she whispered.

"Why?"

Carmen's face scrunched up in disbelief. "Are you serious?" She leaned closer to Emmie, whispering. "That girl we followed isn't even here. Secret organization? This might be some type of cult."

"We're here now. It would be weird if we just got up and left. Besides, she mentioned Jean. She might know something about her. This can be our chance to find her."

Carmen sighed. "Okay, but I have a bad feeling about this. I think we're just wasting our time."

After Mr. Johnson left, Emmie and Carmen continued working on their applications. When Emmie finished filling out the form, she glanced around the room to scope out the competition. There was a diverse group of students. One young man standing at the front writing his name on the completion list appeared to be seven feet tall, while a young lady walking toward the back of the room appeared to be only four feet tall. Some students sat quietly while making nervous body movements, such as leg taps, while others introduced themselves and chatted with others.

A young man with a slender, muscular build sporting a blond buzz cut approached Emmie and Carmen. "Hi ladies. So, are you ready to go to war and tackle the anti-Xeno forces?"

Carmen gasped as her eyes widened. "War?"

The man chuckled. "I'm just messing with you. Don't worry. Students don't do any frontline work."

"Wait, is this some type of military group?" Carmen asked.

The young man slid out a chair and sat down next to Carmen. "Your referral didn't brief you? We're not affiliated with the military. We just work protecting Xeno. Everyone has different tasks depending on their strengths. Some people do computer network security, while others might act as a covert bodyguard. I believe there are other jobs as well. By the way, I'm Marc."

Emmie leaned forward. "Hi Marc. I'm Emmie and she's Carmen. How did ya hear about this organization?'

"From my parents. They work for them and I grew up knowing many Xeno. What about you ladies?"

"Our roommate Jean…"

A voice boomed through a microphone. "Marc Rayments."

"I guess I'm up. It was nice meeting you ladies," Marc said as he stood.

Carmen ogled Marc as he sauntered away. "I would love to know more about him."

Emmie leaned close to Carmen. "Do you think Jean's Xeno DNA is why that girl was looking for her?" she whispered.

Carmen shrugged. "How would she know anything about her test results?"

"I don't know, but I believe we're on the right track."

14

The Doctor's Prescription

Jean woke up to a crick in her neck and shoulders. Her body ached as she stretched her arms. *Maybe I should have let Jamal have the air mattress. Surely, the sofa would have been more comfortable.* She could withstand extreme temperatures, but the attack and sleeping on an uncomfortable air mattress caused every muscle in her body to ache. Kale insisted on putting her and Jamal up for the night at his cramped apartment. She wouldn't have gotten much rest in a five-star hotel bed either. Thoughts about what Dr. Gravin would reveal about her parents and her heritage clattered through her head all night.

Jean glanced around the apartment. Graffiti-style art adorned the walls and the simplistic, modern furniture appeared weathered. Jean couldn't help but wonder if he had snagged most of it from a garage sale. Several tattoo magazines littered the coffee table. Jean grabbed one and began flipping through the pages.

"You don't look too good. Are you okay?" Kale asked as he stood in the kitchen near something steaming on the counter. "How do you drink your coffee?"

"I don't really drink it." Jean yawned. Her stomach grumbled repeatedly. "Do you have any cereal?"

"It's in the cupboard over there. Hope you're okay with bran flakes."

Jean sighed. "Um, yeah, that's fine."

Jamal peeled open his eyes and sat upright. "That coffee smells good," Jamal said as he walked into the kitchen. "If you don't mind making a quick stop at a fast-food joint, I'll pass on the bran flakes."

"Not a problem," Kale said.

"Jamal, can I borrow your phone? I want to see if I can reach my mom."

"Sure," Jamal said as he handed the phone to Jean.

Jean dialed her mother's number, but the call went straight to voicemail. Then she dialed her father's number. The call also went to voicemail. "That's really strange."

"What's wrong?"

Jean took a deep breath. "For some reason, my parents aren't answering. I'm starting to worry. Is there a callback number I can leave for them?"

"Let's try to reach them later. That's my work phone. I'm not supposed to give out the number."

Jean glanced at Kale with pleading eyes.

Kale shook his head. "I don't give out my number either. Sorry."

Jean sighed. "Ugh, I wish I had memorized my roommates' phone numbers. I promised to call them."

"You're putting too much pressure on yourself, Jean," Kale said gently as he handed her a spoon for her cereal. "Your family and friends are probably worried. Maybe this isn't the right time to search for someone who is nothing to you."

Jean looked up at him, surprised by his words. "Nothing? They mean everything to me. My biological parents are a part of who I am. I wouldn't exist if it weren't for them."

Kale huffed. "It's not like it defines who you are today."

"Maybe you're right," Jean said. "But I can't shake the feeling that there's something I need to know. It's like I need to find the missing part of me."

"Kale, give up, man. She's determined to go," Jamal chimed in.

About an hour later, as the three of them got ready to head out the door, Kale started shuffling around the kitchen. Jean heard the clamor of pots and pans and cabinet doors opening and closing. "Kale, are you ready? I would like to get there early. Hopefully, he won't be too busy." Jean and Jamal stood by the door.

"Um, okay." Kale sighed and continued fidgeting around in the kitchen.

Jamal peeked into the kitchen. "Hey, Kale, are you coming?"

Kale sighed. "Where'd they go?" Kale mumbled.

"What's wrong?" Jamal asked.

"I can't find my keys. I know they're here somewhere." Kale continued searching around the kitchen. "Look, if I can't find them, I'll pay for a taxi."

"Let me help." Jamal started looking inside drawers and cabinets. He found the keys perched snugly behind cereal boxes. "Here they are," he said as he tossed them to Kale.

Kale, Jean, and Jamal headed to Dr. Gravin's office in Kale's shabby black truck. Jean sat with Kale in the front, while Jamal sat in the back along with some art supplies and tattoo-related gear. "Man, I really miss my bike," he muttered after something banged his shin when Kale took a rough turn.

Kale wasn't the talkative type, and Jean was too tense about the impending meeting with the doctor to chat. Alt-rock music blared from the radio. "Do you mind?" asked Jean, pointing to the radio.

"No, turn it to what you want."

Jean turned off the music.

Kale stopped by the nearest drive-thru restaurant which was a local chain Jean had never heard of before. Jamal ordered two egg and cheese English muffin sandwiches and orange juice. "Jean, do you want anything? My treat," Jamal said.

"Um, no. That's okay." Jean caught a whiff of bacon and other delicious smells. "Well, if you insist, maybe I'll have the egg, bacon, and cheese sandwich."

Jamal chuckled. "Now, I'm not forcing you to get something."

They arrived at Dr. Gravin's clinic, an unremarkable brown building, made more so by being next to a colorful hipster cafe. The receptionist looked up when the three of them entered and raised one of her thinly penciled eyebrows at Jean. "Can I help you?"

"Uh, yeah. Is Dr. Gravin in? He treated my mother so, um, I wanted a follow-up with him about that."

"Do you have an appointment?"

Jean glanced at Kale. "Um, no. Sorry."

The receptionist rolled her eyes. "I'll have to see if he's available. Have a seat. We don't usually have time for walk-ins. Make sure you make an appointment next time."

Jean couldn't stop her leg from bobbing up and down, and soon someone's hand wrapped around hers.

"Nervous much?" asked Jamal. "I'm not judging or anything. I know it's a big deal for you."

"It is, yeah." Jean paused to collect her thoughts for a bit. "You know, you didn't have to come in with us. But I'm glad you did."

Jamal shrugged. "Now, I'm curious to see how this all turns out. And I could never leave a damsel in distress, even if she's not in so much distress anymore."

Jean giggled. "Really? I'm a damsel now?"

Jamal moved his lips into a crooked grin. At that moment, the receptionist appeared and escorted them to a small room.

"Come in, come in, please have a seat," said a nerdy, yet friendly voice. Its owner was a weathered and balding man wearing a gaudy, gold-flecked tie highlighting a mismatched ensemble of clothing. His movements were stiff as he gestured toward empty chairs. "So, what can I do to help you?"

Kale should start since he knows his mother was a patient. Jean looked at Kale. *Why isn't he saying anything? Well, I guess I have no choice but to say something if I don't want to be here all day.* "Um, Dr. Gravin, my name is Jean Anderson, and this is my half-brother, Kale. We were in the foster care system at an early age, so we don't know much about our biological parents. Kale said his birth mother came to you for treatment and I thought that maybe my birth mother did as well. We just want to find out what we can about them, especially our father. We thought you might have some information."

Dr. Gravin rested his chin on his fingers once she was done and peered at Jean over the top rim of his glasses.

"I am sure the three of you are aware of patient confidentiality and the privacy laws we must follow. I need consent from patients before I release their information to a third party. And in your case, you don't even know for certain that your mothers *were* patients here. There's a strong possibility that I never treated them."

"No, my mom definitely came to you," said Kale. "My birth record information lists your name as her doctor."

"I'm sure you think so, Mr. Kale. However, that doesn't count as definitive proof."

Jean and Kale glanced at each other. "Can you see if you have their names on file?" asked Jean, half desperate and half annoyed. "I took a DNA test that proves I'm related to a Mary Galloway. She's listed as my mother. Kale also has a DNA test proving his relationship to his birth mother."

"And if you *do* have them as patients, then direct family members can request their information on their behalf if the patients are unable to do so themselves," said Jamal. "In fact, if you withhold this information, you can be sued for misuse of privacy laws by a good lawyer. If you want, I can call my attorney so you can speak to him right now." Jamal winked at Jean.

The doctor's face blanched a bit at Jamal's revelation, but he quickly recovered. "Fine, I suppose I can at least check our records for their names. Did you say Mary? And what was the other name? And please give me a rough timeline of their visits to this clinic."

"Mary Galloway," said Jean. Dr. Gravin's eyes glimmered with recognition. "She would have come to this clinic at least eighteen years ago."

"And my mom, Melanie Daniels, would have come twenty-nine years ago," Kale said.

"Ah yes, Mary Galloway. That name rings a bell, at least. I don't remember Ms. Daniels, but I can check our records." He started by searching his computer, then shuffled to a filing cabinet and continued his search there. "Many of our older records are kept in an offsite storage facility, but there may be some information in our backup records. I'll be right back." The doctor left the office.

"Is all that legal stuff you said true?" Jean whispered to Jamal as the doctor searched his cabinet.

Jamal chuckled and leaned close to Jean's ear. "Hell if I know. I *do* have an excellent lawyer, though."

"Jamal!"

"Hey, it worked, didn't it?"

The doctor returned to the office holding two files. "I believe I have something here, yes. Files for one Melanie Daniels and one Mary Galloway." Dr. Gravin sighed as he flipped through the files. "Both have the same paternal code. The father was a man named Azon. I'm sure most of my information is outdated."

Jean's heart leaped. She was about to find out more about her birth parents than she had ever known before. But the doctor's follow-up made her heart plunge back down again.

"Unfortunately, there's not much relevant information to help in your search. Melanie Daniels had endometriosis, while we diagnosed Mary Galloway with an ovulation disorder. We treated both with our Juno package, which includes a collection of alternative remedies and medicines sanctioned by the laws of good practice in Seattle. Both underwent in vitro fertilization. Oh, there's a note in the Mary Galloway file. I lost contact with her just before she was due to give birth. Ah, that's right, I remember her. She practically disappeared into thin air. I couldn't find a trace of either her or her baby. Well, I suppose the latter has now been accounted for."

Dr. Gravin smiled faintly at Jean, although she didn't notice him with the storm of emotions in her mind. Jamal snatched the files from the doctor. "Is that really all you have, Doc?" Jamal started flipping through the folders. "What about Jean's father? Where's that information?"

"What do you think we are, the FBI? We're a fertility clinic," Dr. Gravin huffed. "And these are very old cases you're inquiring about. Besides, a name like Azon isn't very common, either as a first name or a surname. I'm sure you have plenty of resources you can make use of to find out more about him. But he wasn't a patient here, so you won't find much about him in our database. There's nothing more to be said."

Kale shoved his chair back with a jerk. "Then I guess we're done here. Thanks, Dr. Gravin. Nice meeting you. Come on, guys, let's go."

Jean slowly arose from her chair. *That was a waste of time. Well, at least I got to meet my brother.* As she extended her hand to thank Dr. Gravin for his time, her eyes drifted to his tie. That's when she saw it. Lost among the flecks of gold on the tie was a tie pin. It was a golden scythe—the exact same one she'd seen on Agent Smyte. She jerked her hand back in shock and whispered to Jamal. "He's with them! The men who tried to kidnap me!"

Jamal rushed toward Dr. Gravin. The doctor slid a syringe from inside his coat sleeve and raised his arm, aiming the syringe toward Jamal's arm. Jamal shimmied to the side, grabbed the doctor's wrist, twisted it with a deft flick, and pierced the doctor with the syringe. Dr. Gravin grunted in pain as the pale green contents of the syringe flooded his veins. He scrambled toward a small wooden box on the shelf behind him, but Kale jumped in front of him while Jamal shoved him. Kale grabbed the box and pulled out a navy blue syringe from inside it. Dr. Gravin stumbled back into his chair, choking and coughing from the effects of the green liquid.

"So, what do we have here?" Kale said, waving the blue syringe in front of the doctor. "Hmm ... is this the antidote, Doctor? Is this what you're reaching for?" asked Kale casually as the doctor trembled and struggled to breathe. Kale leaned close to the doctor's face. "What was in that syringe? Cyanide?"

The doctor nodded and reached his arm toward Kale. "Please, I beg you ... the antidote..."

Jamal sat in the guest chair and propped his legs onto the doctor's desk. "Maybe if you help us, we'll help you. Jean, tell the doctor what you want."

Jean trembled. "Tell me about my parents, Dr. Gravin. And tell me the truth this time."

The doctor gasped in fits and spurts until Kale injected a sliver of the antidote, just enough for the doctor to become coherent.

The doctor took a deep breath and sighed. "You want the truth? Fine! During my work as a fertility specialist, I conducted genomic research. I made great advances in my thirty years of work. Advances in science and medicine that will make humans more resistant to cancers and environmental problems. Advances in science that will make—"

Jamal flung his legs off the desk. "Stick to the point, Doc, or you're not getting the rest of the antidote."

"You young people are so impatient these days," the doctor exclaimed with a raspy voice. "I spent most of my life as a clinical geneticist, and the bulk of my research focused on merging human DNA with that of the Sepids." The doctor tilted his head back as he gasped for air between each word. "It wasn't easy merging the DNA of two different species. It took a lot of trial and error."

"Doctor, please, what does that have to do with me?" Jean exclaimed.

"That's what I'm trying to explain. Using various genetic engineering methods, we successfully merged DNA from the Sepids' sperm with DNA in human eggs from the fertility clinic. Genesis Sector has very advanced labs. After confirming fertilization and the embryo has reached the blastocyst stage—"

"I don't want a science lesson," interrupted Jean, and Dr. Gravin grumpily paused. "What do you mean by 'the Sepids'?"

"That is what we called the aliens we experimented on."

"Say what?" Jamal backed away in shock and gave Jean a curious look. "What do you mean, aliens? The ones from outer space? Little green men and all that? You're joking, right?"

Jean realized only then that until that point, she hadn't mentioned anything about her and Kale's alien origins to Jamal. She shot Jamal an apologetic look. "Why do you call them Sepids?"

"That is what we called them when I joined Genesis Sector. I assume it has something to do with some similarities they have with cuttlefish, which belong to the order *Sepiida* in the animal kingdom."

"And what is Genesis Sector? Is that the group you and Agent Smyte work for?"

The doctor took a ragged breath and cleared his throat, as though preparing for a long speech. "You must know that with climate change worsening by the year and the increasing rates of cancer, it has become harder for humans to survive on this planet. Soon, it may well be impossible. Years ago, in anticipation of this outcome, the government sanctioned a secret organization called Genesis Sector. The purpose of Genesis Sector is to find a way for humans to survive the worst outcomes of global warming and the most deadly diseases. I was in the genetics subdivision of Genesis Sector. We have known about the existence of the Sepids, and their abilities, for decades now. My job was to find a way to evolve humankind by genetically mingling human DNA with that of the Sepids with the end goal of making humans stronger and more resistant to illness and environmental changes. And if we can eliminate diseases like cancer, everyone benefits."

"That's awful," said Jean. "You're messing around with fate." She glanced at Dr. Gravin. His face seemed to become redder with every second.

"It's not all bad. Wouldn't it be great if his work leads to less suffering?" Kale asked.

"Right. My work benefits humanity," spat Dr. Gravin before he coughed non-stop. His hands trembled as he lifted a mug to his mouth and took a couple of gulps of water. "Whether the planet burns or endures a new ice age, humans are not genetically equipped to survive such harsh conditions."

Jamal cocked his head. "I still don't understand. What does this have to do with Jean?"

"Jean is a product of our research," the doctor said, staring at Jean as he lifted a brow. "Extreme heat and cold don't bother you, do they? You must have noticed it by now. And perhaps you have heightened senses? Or an innate resistance to physical injury? You possess these powers because of your Sepid DNA."

Jean's mouth gaped slightly open as the blood seemed to flow from her face. "So you experimented on my mother?"

"Well, not directly. We created the modified embryos from your mother's eggs and those of many others. In the beginning, we weren't successful and lost a lot of embryos. We were able to perfect the technique and eventually achieve a 90% success rate."

Jamal stood and paced. "Wait a minute. Are you saying Jean is half alien? I didn't realize she was one of the..."

Why does he keep interrupting? Jean held up her hand in front of Jamal. "Doctor, where's my mother? Is she still alive?"

Doctor Gravin sighed. "I wasn't lying before when I said I lost contact with her just before you were born. We retrieved your mother's eggs and fertilized them in vitro with the Sepid sperm. I believe there were about five embryos from your mother's eggs. We scheduled an appointment to implant two of the embryos into your mother and each of our research gestational carriers. We only implanted two embryos into your mother and one of the research carriers, Caroline Archer, before the remaining embryos were stolen."

"So, Jean has more siblings?" Jamal asked.

Jean rolled her eyes in exasperation. "Let the doctor continue," she huffed.

The doctor leaned forward, gasping for air and almost falling to the floor. Jamal rushed over to the doctor and caught him before he landed on the floor. "Thank you."

"Does he need another dose?" Jean asked.

Kale jabbed the doctor in his thigh with the antidote filled syringe. "Go on doctor. Continue."

The doctor took a deep breath and cleared his throat. As he spoke, his voice was so slow and monotone, Jean was scared he was going to fall asleep or pass out any minute. "I don't know what happened to the missing embryos. Our original plan was to keep Mary as a patient and refer her to our pediatrician so that we could observe your progress as you grew up in the outside world. The research gestational carriers agreed to surrender the babies to us as soon as they were born. Unfortunately, Caroline sought to undermine our operation. She stole many of our files, along with a case full of frozen embryos, and escaped from our facility. We later discovered that Caroline was an undercover operative from a rival organization. We also lost contact with Mary. She seemed to disappear into thin air."

"Wait, one heavily pregnant woman outsmarted a whole government agency like that?" asked Jamal, the admiration evident in his voice. "She must have been a real badass."

This is starting to sound like a spy drama and not the glamorous kind I'd like to be in either, Jean thought to herself as the doctor frowned at Jamal before continuing.

"Eventually, we were able to track your mother down. Unlike Caroline, she wasn't trained in the art of evading our investigative measures. While we never found Caroline again, we *did* intercept your mother. Of course, Mary claimed she had no idea where you were—that blasted Caroline had prepared for such a contingency—and so we have been searching for you and the others born from the stolen embryos ever since. As for your mother, I don't know what happened after Genesis Sector's agents interrogated her. I assume they made sure she wouldn't be a problem in the future."

"Do you mean ... they killed her?" Jean's eyes widened.

The doctor simply shrugged. "As I told you, I don't know. She was no longer relevant to my research, so I didn't care to find out. Anyway, I wasn't privy to that information."

"Real ray of sunshine, aren't you?" quipped Kale.

Jean glanced at Kale before turning back to Dr. Gravin. "What about Kale? Have you been looking for him too?"

The doctor glared at Kale. "When he was born, we still hadn't perfected the merging process. The mixture was still not there yet, still suboptimal. He didn't have all the qualities we wanted. But with you, Miss Anderson, we finally got it right. We were able to inject twelve percent more Sepid DNA into your genetic makeup compared to your brother. And that made you the perfect merging of the two species.

That's why we continued to search for you and your missing twin. We also don't know what became of the stolen embryos and research files."

"Did you hear that, Kale?" Dr. Gravin turned to an increasingly irritated Kale as Jean struggled to process everything she had just heard. "You're less than second-rate compared to your sister. How does it feel to be an experimental reject?"

"Piss off!" Kale raised his fist and swung it toward the doctor's smug face, but Jamal grabbed his wrist, stopping him just in time.

Dr. Gravin coughed weakly as the cyanide in his blood continued to take its toll.

Jean continued her interrogation as the flurry of activity jerked her back into the present. "Is my father Azon still alive? And where is he?"

"Azon is still alive, yes. His DNA is far too important to our research. As for his location..." Dr. Gravin went silent.

"This isn't the time to be coy, Doctor," threatened Kale, dangling the antidote precariously from his fingers.

"I believe Azon is still being held at the Genesis Sector facility here in Washington state. It's hidden in the forests around the base of Mt. Adams, but you'll never find it on a map. And even if you did, the security—"

"Yeah, we get the picture, Doc," said Jamal, shoving him forcefully to shut him up.

Kale turned toward Jean. "I can tell what you're thinking, Jean, and I can't believe I'm saying this, but I'm siding with the doctor on this one. The place will be heavily guarded, and we're just three people. It's too dangerous."

"Kale, Azon is our *father*. He's the only bio parent we have left! We need to rescue him. They're treating him like some sort of lab rat." Jean's voice had a steel edge to it as she stared at Kale with pleading eyes.

Jamal nodded his head in support.

"You do realize your life will be at risk if we do this?" Kale asked.

Jean sighed. "I need to do this. Besides, we'll have Jamal with us. He's really strong. He fought a lot of men at once and saved my life."

Kale sighed. "Fine, but you're coming along for the ride, sunshine," he said as he jabbed the remaining antidote hard into Dr. Gravin's leg. "And don't even *think* of giving us any wrong directions if you value your life. I'm taking the remaining cyanide for good measure."

Jamal peeked out the office door. A tall young woman stood at the inside front desk, speaking with the receptionist. "Let's wait until the hallway is clear before we leave. Doc, is there a back door?"

"Uh, yeah," Dr. Gravin said as he gently massaged his leg.

"I'll go out first and distract the lady at the desk by telling her I need to schedule an appointment."

Jamal grinned. "Great idea, Jean. You can go out the front and we'll leave with the doctor out the back door."

After the patient at the front desk left, Jean approached the receptionist. "Hello, I need to schedule a follow-up appointment with the doctor."

"Okay, the doctor didn't bring your chart. I'll go grab it."

"Oh, that's okay. I forgot I need to check my schedule. Can you give me a list of possible dates and times? I'll call back as soon as I get home."

"Sure."

As soon as the receptionist turned toward her computer, Jean glanced in Jamal's direction and nodded. Jamal and Kale quickly led Dr. Gravin out the back exit.

15

Emmie's Test

Emmie and Carmen clutched stacks of flyers featuring Jean's smiling face and walked through the bustling quad, pausing to pin flyers to cluttered bulletin boards, signposts, and trees. A crisp wind fought to steal the flyers from their hands.

Emmie approached a small group of students chatting while sitting on the lawn. "Excuse me," she said, leaning down and handing them a flyer. "My roommate is missing. Have you seen her?" The students dropped the flyer on the ground, shook their heads, and returned to their conversations. Emmie turned toward Carmen. "No one cares. Their fellow student is missin', and they couldn't care less," she huffed.

"They don't know her like we do. Besides, this is a large campus. What are the odds they would see her even if she wasn't missing? I don't think there's a good chance we'll find her this way."

"Are you saying you wanna quit?"

"I'm not saying we should quit. At least, not yet. I'm saying that we should be realistic and not expect to find her by handing out flyers. I mean, do you really think she is wandering around campus after being in a horrific car crash? I don't think so," Carmen said.

"You can't be sure who may have information. Maybe another student witnessed the accident. Or perhaps she's roaming around campus after sufferin' from amnesia because of the car accident."

Carmen chuckled. "Really? You don't really believe that, do you?"

"I'm just sayin', you never know what you'll find," Emmie said as she shoved a flyer at a student passing by her. The other student batted his arm at the flyer, forcing it to float through the air. "We won't find anything if we don't look."

"I don't mind looking. I just think we need to adjust our expectations."

After canvassing for a couple of hours, Emmie received an email notification on her phone from the Starlight Organization. She read the notification and smiled. "It looks like I made the cut."

Carmen scrunched her brows. "The cut?"

"Yeah, check your email. I just received a link from that secret society to schedule my health exams. Tell me which date you prefer. Then we can go together."

Carmen slid her phone out of her stylish leather purse and scanned her email messages. "I don't see anything. Maybe they didn't select me for the next step."

"Check your Spam folder."

"I did. Nothing's there."

"They might not have notified everyone at the same time. Keep checking."

Carmen sighed. "I wonder why they didn't pick me."

"Just keep checking your email." Emmie was excited about the opportunity to join the Starlight Organization's student group. As she scheduled her health exams, she noticed an option to consent to an "enhanced evaluation." Curious, she checked the box, wondering if it had anything to do with the strange tech she glimpsed at the interview. She couldn't wait to see what was in store for her and if it could lead her to Jean's whereabouts.

———— ❈ ————

The next morning, Emmie went to a small medical office to complete her physical and psychological evaluation. A nurse led her to a sterile exam room containing advanced medical equipment with blinking lights and transparent screens displaying streaming data. After standard tests, the nurse pulled out a metallic device. "This will assess your biology on a microscopic level while gathering baseline neurochemistry readings," she explained, pressing it gently to Emmie's neck.

Emmie flinched as a cold sensation spread under her skin. Foreign-looking graphics of her nervous system materialized on a screen. The nurse added, "We need to fully analyze a recruit's capacities if they want to synchronize with next-gen augmentation gear."

After psych evaluations came the fitness tests. The machines were unlike any gym tech Emmie had ever seen. Sleek biometric sensors mapped her body as she jogged on a treadmill with floating inline skates. They had her wear a flexible suit that enabled full-motion holographic tracking of her muscle movements during strength tests.

Walking back alone, Emmie gazed up at the first faint stars winking into view. She smiled, imagining herself saving aliens from the evils of the world. But with a start, she realized she left her room so quickly, she forgot her mobile device. Her steps slowed, smile fading. For all the exciting possibilities opening up from this opportunity, Emmie hoped she wouldn't completely lose touch with the people she already cared about most. She staggered back to the dorm, where Carmen was busy studying. "Any news?"

Carmen rolled her eyes. "No."

Emmie dragged herself up to her bed. "What's wrong with you?"

"Nothing. I'm glad they didn't pick me. I enjoy having my weekends free," Carmen said, tossing her hair. "Are you sure you really want to do this? I was looking at some stuff online about Xenos and alien abductions. It's really scary. You should read this one guy's story. I'm going to send you a link. He was kept aboard a spaceship for five hours being poked and prodded."

Emmie chuckled. "He was probably dreamin'."

"No, it's true. I'm going to send you the link."

"Don't bother. At first, I wasn't sure I was interested, but now I really think I'll enjoy being a member. I'm definitely intrigued by the whole mysteriousness of it, but those exams were intense. They took so much blood and they even had me do one of those inkblot tests." Emmie plopped down onto a chair. "Oh, I forgot to tell you. I spoke with one of the other applicants about Jean. She believes the organization may be protectin' her, but she doesn't know for sure because everything is so top secret.

"Well, I really need to study," Carmen said dryly, with her eyes focused on her laptop.

"Okay. Oh, I almost forgot. I'm supposed to meet Dawn and Todd for dinner, anyway."

"Who?" Carmen asked, casting the slightest glance toward Emmie before returning her gaze to her laptop.

"Oh, they're a couple of students I met while taking tests for the organization. Have fun studying. Bye, roomie." Emmie hopped up and left the room.

As Emmie strolled toward her dinner meeting, a warm anticipation filled her heart. The vibrant campus lights illuminated the quad, casting a colorful glow on her path. The gentle breeze whispered through her hair, carrying the scent of fresh blossoms from nearby gardens. Excitement tingled in her fingertips as she yearned for the possibility of forging new connections. Yet, deep within, she cherished the familiar warmth of old friendships, not wanting to let them slip away.

16

Into the Genesis Den

Jean, Jamal, Kale, and Dr. Gravin set off for the Genesis Sector base in Kale's van. Kale and Jean sat in front, while Jamal kept an eye on a bound Dr. Gravin in the back. Dr. Gravin was positioned so that he had a view of the road in front and could give directions when Kale barked at him for them.

Any other day, Jean might have gazed wistfully at the thick forests they drove past after leaving the city limits of Seattle. They glowed enchantingly in the warm hues of the setting sun's light. Emmie would have squealed at the chance to go trekking among the trees here or to climb some of the gentler slopes in the region. Jean wondered how she and Carmen were faring back in Montana. Maybe when this was all over, they could come back here for a much-needed vacation.

Jean idly switched the radio channel to something with less twangy country guitars in it.

It was already nightfall when the Genesis Sector base finally came into view. As Dr. Gravin had mentioned, it was indeed well hidden behind a fake mountain wall that reached 1000 feet high and was covered with a variety of realistic-looking foliage. The base was impressive, given the extensive area it occupied. The buildings inside were blocky and modern-looking and stood at odds with the tall fir trees that grew outside the boundary walls of the complex.

A pair of guards carefully watched the main gateway into the complex in a small security booth. Kale switched off his lights before parking the van in a small clearing surrounded by cedars and pines. From there, they had a clear view of the entrance to the facility while safely hidden by the cover of the trees and the darkness. They were also far enough from the complex to be out of range of any searchlights it might have. When the engine finally stopped whirring, Kale turned toward the rest of them.

"We should be safe here. I'm going to recon the perimeter, and I'll take Dr. Sunshine along with me in case I have questions. Can you two stay with the van until I'm back?"

"Yeah, I think we'll be fine," said Jean, getting out from her seat to stretch her legs. "You go on ahead."

Jamal and Kale quickly untied Dr. Gravin before Kale dragged him off into the trees toward the complex. Jamal watched them go until they were out of sight and then sat in the doorway to the back of the van.

"Brrr, it sure gets frosty out in these forests at night, huh? It's a good thing I brought along some extra layers." He reached into the van and grabbed one jacket he had with him, before remembering that Jean wouldn't need one. Sighing, Jamal lamented, "Some people have all the luck."

Jean looked at her hands. They were already approaching the fiery color of the sunset they had just driven through. She glanced at Jamal. His mouth hung open as he focused his eyes on her hands.

Jamal grinned. "So, you're half-alien, huh? I was wondering why they…"

"What? Why they what?"

"Nothing. It's not important."

Jean sighed. "I'm sorry I didn't tell you about it before. It's just, I couldn't make it sound right in my head, you know? I mean, how do you just tell people you're some kind of alien-human hybrid? And I ... I didn't want you to think I was crazy or something." She turned away, twirling a strand of her hair.

Jamal gazed at the facility entrance for a bit. Then he chuckled. "I mean, there's a slight chance I would have taken you to an asylum instead of Capitol Hill if you'd told me that. But things are starting to add up better now. Those men at the crash who were after you, your skin changing color when things get a little chilly, the stuff that Doc was saying ... it's still crazy, yeah, but it's a kind of crazy that makes sense, you know what I'm saying?"

Jean giggled. "Not really, but I think I do, yeah."

"Hey, Jean, listen. I'm guessing you haven't told too many people about this. But if you want to really vent, to just get it all out there, well, I'm willing to hear you. And I'm sure the woodland critters around here won't mind, either."

Jean thought about it. He had a point; she had been bottling up everything she had been through in the last few days. And they'd only known each other for a few days, but in that time, he'd saved her life at least once and helped her find out the truth about Azon and her mother. If there was anyone she could confide in, if only to help sort out the tangle of thoughts in her excited brain, it would be Jamal. It also helped that he was easy to talk to. *And I kind of like his look*, she thought with a smirk.

So Jean told him everything about the series of events that had occurred ever since Professor Higgins had her class take that fateful DNA test back in Montana. She described the incident with Krenik and Ziva, the revelations from the DNA test results, and the drive to Seattle, which ended in the crash.

"The reason I decided to major in genealogy and family history is because I was adopted. I mean, don't get me wrong, ever since Iris and Grant Anderson took me in, they have been the kindest and most loving parents I could ever want. No matter what I find out on this journey, they'll always be my mom and dad. But before them, I was just another foster kid drifting in the system, moving from home to home, and it sucked that I didn't know where I came from."

"Even now, knowing about Azon and Mary Galloway and Genesis Sector, I still feel a bit incomplete. I wanted to become a genealogist so I could help other families find out where their roots were, so their lives wouldn't suck like my years in foster care did. It might sound sappy and cheesy to some people, but it's true." Jean's gaze landed on Jamal, waiting for his signature wisecrack or the sight of his trademark crooked grin. But he was oddly silent, as though he had been properly listening throughout her recounting of events, so she continued.

"And now I'm about to find out about the alien part of my heritage. When I was a kid, I used to get bullied because people said my eyes glowed funny or my skin changed to odd colors. I didn't know what they were talking about. When I looked in the mirror, everything seemed fine. I mean, everyone looks a little different in the sun, right? Other kids called me a mutant freak. And I hated that part of me; I used to think it was all wrong. That *I* was all wrong. But now, if I can finally see what my father is truly like, what his side of my genetic lineage is like ... it will feel *right*, this time. And I will feel right, for a change." Jean stopped to deeply breathe in the crisp forest air.

Jamal waited for her to slow down a little more before quietly chipping in. "I don't really know what to say. You've had it rough. Damn,

I wouldn't want to be in your shoes, alien powers or no. But at least things are looking up now, right?"

Jean glanced at him again. He was just accepting everything she said. No quips, no judgment, no doubts. She had to admit that she liked this side of him, even if it was temporary. "You can walk away at any time, Jamal. This isn't your family we're finding answers about. This isn't your fight against Genesis Sector."

Jamal chuckled. "Um, no. How would you fight off a group of big bad men without me?" Jamal chuckled. "Besides, I'd get lost in the woods real quick if I walked away now."

"Hey, I'm serious! I appreciate your help and all, but you could be relaxing at home instead of sneaking into Genesis."

Jamal stared into the distance. Then he softly spoke. "When I was young, like, *really* young, the government shipped my dad off to some war in the Middle East. Maybe it was Iraq or Iran, I don't know. Point is, he never came back. My mom got some of his things when the soldiers came to tell us he was killed in action, but a bunch of trinkets could never replace him. I guess I know what it's like to not have a father in my life and to not have a family that feels complete."

The sound of something rustling in the wind filled the air, and moments later, Kale and Dr. Gravin returned.

"Kale, how does it look?" Jean asked.

"It should be pretty easy to get in. The doc and I will go through the security gate in the truck. You and Jamal run along the right side of the truck. I'll try to distract the guards so you can sneak in. There are a bunch of tall weeds. Hide there. I'll text Jamal when it's safe to come out."

A little while later, Jean gazed out the window as the van slowly rumbled toward the entrance to the complex. Her breath stalled when it reached the glaring lights at the entrance and slowed to a halt. A muscular security guard approached the driver's window while another one watched from the booth.

Kale flashed the syringe with the green liquid at Dr. Gravin and nodded his head. "No funny stuff, Doc. These people won't care if you're dead or alive."

Dr. Gravin rolled down his window. "I'm Dr. Jenson Gravin, Associate Director of the Apollo Project. Here's my identification," said the doctor from the passenger's seat in front. "This young man is with me. He's my assistant from the clinic."

The guard slid a palm-sized tablet from his pocket and tapped the screen. After reading its contents, he leaned forward, peering into the vehicle. "I don't have you on my list for today."

"I know." Dr. Gravin cleared his throat. "Uh, this wasn't a planned visit. I'm sorry for not calling first. I need to finish the medical testing. They want reports tomorrow morning."

The guard shined a small, bright flashlight on both Dr. Gravin's and Kale's IDs to examine them. He then took out a scanner from his chest pocket and scanned the doctor's right eye, followed by Kale's. After looking at the iris scanner readout for confirmation, he pocketed it and said, "I need to confirm that it's okay for you to come in without being on today's list. You know we have strict protocols."

"I understand."

The guard stepped away from the truck and spoke with someone on his cellphone. Several minutes later, he returned. "We'll need to search your vehicle, Dr. Gravin." He then motioned to the other guard to head toward the back of the van.

"Of course, we have nothing to hide," said the doctor with his weak smile.

"Hey, unlock the door," called out the second guard.

"Oh right, that door jams a bit, hang on," said Kale, as he opened his door and started climbing down from his seat.

The first guard slid a gun out of his holster and aimed it toward Kale. "Don't get out," he yelled.

Kale rotated back to a sitting position in his seat and shut his door. "Fine, just give it a sharp tug at the handle. Try not to break it, okay?"

When the two guards finally yanked the door open, the second guard climbed into the back space of the van and examined its contents. After he climbed out again, he gave a curt signal to the first guard, who said, "Alright, you can go in," before letting the van through the entranceway.

The van crawled toward the parking lot and stopped in a spot that was less lit up by streetlamps. After Kale and Dr. Gravin got out of the van, they stood there for a while, Kale checking for patrolling guards while Dr. Gravin glanced at his watch. As soon as all the guards left, Kale sent a text to Jamal.

Jean and Jamal sprinted to where Kale and the doctor stood.

Kale grinned. "Good, you made it."

"Yeah, the distraction with the van's jammed door helped," said Jean, while Jamal surveyed the area. "Are you guys sure that part of the entrance we snuck through wasn't covered by cameras?" she asked.

Dr. Gravin coughed and cleared his throat. "The security cameras normally point away from the guards while they're in their post, so I don't believe they have them aimed there."

"Enough with the chitchat. We need to hurry before someone sees us," Kale said, grabbing the doctor and pushing him forward. "Alright, Dr. Sunshine, which way?"

After giving Kale a withering look, the doctor led them toward the biggest building just ahead of them. But instead of going to the bright and glassy area that was the main entrance, he led them along the left side of the building, past a few more cars and some heavier vehicles to what eventually ended up being a side entrance. Dr. Gravin then pulled out a card on a lanyard he was wearing. He swiped the card against a detector near the entrance, which unlocked the door.

"This is the entrance the maintenance staff uses," said Dr. Gravin as they followed him inside. "Most of them should be back in their living quarters at this time. If we continue along this service corridor, we will soon find ourselves in the elevator lobby, where we can access the research floors."

"No elevators for us, though," said Kale.

Jamal nodded in agreement. "Yeah, we don't want to announce ourselves. You should be fine with a few flights of stairs, right, Doc?"

The doctor grumbled in agreement.

True to Dr. Gravin's word, the drab, shabbily lit service corridor soon gave way to the much sleeker heart of the main building. Jean had to inhale sharply at the sight of it. The walls and furnishings gleamed with the cold glare of a pristine corporate building, and the few potted plants that gave the place a semblance of life were artificial. The sharp fluorescent lighting only served to make the place feel that much more sterile as it reflected off the spotless walls and the dark tiled floor.

Jean kept her steps light as she followed Dr. Gravin, Kale, and Jamal through the stark halls. *Too easy*, whispered a voice in Jean's mind. Her pulse quickened and her senses prickled with unease.

The bare concrete walls leeched all warmth from the narrow space. Few decorations and furnishings occupied the gloomy space. Jean took another deep breath. The air was heavy and stale. *We can do this*, she reassured herself. *We've come this far, and we can finish this thing.*

Dr. Gravin gave the silvery elevator doors one last longing look before leading them to the emergency stairwell. The time had come to descend into the lion's den.

We're coming for you, Azon. And we're going to get you out of here.

17

The Fifteenth Door

Jean thought back to the time during her English Lit class in high school when she had to read Dante's *Divine Comedy*. She barely made it through the first book, *Inferno*. Most of the details were lost from her memory, but she recalled that most of that book was about Dante slowly descending through the nine circles of Hell. *I wonder if I'm going down my own circles of Hell now.*

At least one person she was with might have agreed with her. Dr. Gravin was already panting by the time they exited the first stairwell. "We have to walk through this corridor to reach a set of stairs in a different area of the building," he said, leaning against a wall for a breather.

"Fine, but remember to avoid the main hallways, okay?" said Jamal.

Dr. Gravin slid down and plopped onto the nearest step. He pulled a handkerchief out of his pocket and dabbed the beads of sweat on his forehead. "I don't know how much longer I can go."

Jamal wrapped his arms under Dr. Gravin's armpits and lifted him up to standing. "We don't have time to rest. Lean on me for support." The doctor's breathing intensified.

"Do you think giving him more of the antidote will help?" Jean asked.

Jamal shrugged. "I already gave him the entire vial. We really need to hurry."

As they walked, an eerie silence hung in the air, devoid of any signs of life. Air-conditioning units whirred at lowered intensity while empty desks were strewn with notepads and piles of documents to be dealt with on another day. The place felt ripe for hunting by some disillusioned office worker.

They reached the next stairwell without incident, although something was bothering Jean, and she couldn't put her finger on it. The next level they walked through resembled a museum gallery more than an office. The lighting was warmer, and the walls were lined with framed documents filled with unrecognizable writing. In a style reminiscent of the alphabets from Jean's Asian Cultures course in college, the letters were written in a loopy and cursive manner. Sleek display cases housed strange artifacts with enigmatic markings. She inspected some of them, hoping to innately recognize something within their structures, but nothing came to mind. "Have you seen anything like these before?" she asked Kale, who shook his head in response.

"They'd make me believe in aliens even if I didn't know everything I do now," commented Jamal. "Any idea what they're for, Doc?"

"Those trifles aren't relevant to my research," Dr. Gravin huffed before moving on.

Another stairwell descent later, they were in a level occupied by science laboratories filled with equipment that looked nearly as alien as the earlier artifacts had. Something about the return to harsh and cold fluorescent lights helped Jean figure out what was bothering her. *This has been way too easy.* She drifted toward Jamal as they followed behind Kale and the doctor.

"Something doesn't feel right," she whispered to him. "Where are all the people? We should have seen someone by now."

Jamal locked eyes with Jean, and she could tell he was thinking the same thing. "I don't know," he said, shaking his head.

As she walked, the hairs on Jean's neck prickled. *We've come too far to turn back now, but...* She strained her ears for any unusual sound—the pounding of footsteps, distant conversations, anything.

Many of the labs they walked past contained diagrams of body parts, like something out of a biology book. They appeared human at first, but when Jean took a closer peek, the proportions and features were wrong. The limbs were stretched and fluid, the shapes of the organs weren't the same, things were in the wrong place—she wished there were some pictures where everything was put together, just so she could get a proper preview of what her father would look like when they saw him.

Jean inhaled deeply to slow her breath. "When did the Sepids come to Earth? And for how long have we known of their existence?" she asked Dr. Gravin.

"We have known about them since the early seventies, not long after the first moon landing. Whether they were here on Earth before that, we don't know. They won't say either."

"I used to think it was strange how the aliens in TV shows could always speak English perfectly after landing here," remarked Jamal, "but I guess that's how they are in real life too?"

"Apparently our efforts to decipher their language are making some headway," said the doctor, "but yes, their grasp of our language is much better than ours of theirs, for the time being. So what little communication we have with them has been in English, unfortunately."

Jamal furrowed his brows. "What do you mean, *unfortunately*?"

"Ah, here we are. Give me a moment."

They had arrived at a door that was thicker and tougher than anything else they had seen inside the building. Made of imposing steel, it looked like something a high-tech bank vault would have. Dr. Gravin again pulled out his card, tapped it on a detector on the side, and entered a passcode into the keypad below it. The door clunked open with a heavy thud.

"Past this door are the specimen containment units," said Dr. Gravin, again stopping for breath. "If I'm not mistaken, Azon should be in unit number fifteen. This is the most secure area in the facility, for obvious reasons. But contrary to how it may appear, the containment units were designed to be as comfortable and accommodating for the Sepid specimens as we can manage."

"They're prisoners in here," said Jean coldly, looking at the steel door. "It doesn't matter how accommodating you are if they don't have their freedom."

Dr. Gravin's forehead glistened with beads of sweat as he leaned against the nearest wall and wiped his head with the back of his hand. "It's really not as bad as it may seem. All their needs are met and they're protected from organizations that don't want them here. People who hunt them and would prefer to see them dead."

Jean rolled her eyes. "Just take us to Azon."

The doors in the passageway beyond were all made of similarly thick, sturdy steel, and had numbered keypads on them as well. Their footsteps echoed as though they were walking inside a crypt, and the dark surroundings added to the oppressive atmosphere. When they reached the fifteenth door from the entrance, Dr. Gravin stopped in front of the keypad and then glanced in their direction, as though asking for permission.

Jamal said, "Go on, open the door." Kale simply nodded.

Jean's pulse soared as she stared at the door. Azon was somewhere behind that impenetrable door. Mere steps away. After all this time, all the revelations and danger, she would finally see her father's true face.

Dr. Gravin sighed with reluctance, then tapped a passcode on the keypad with shaking fingers. The lock to the door opened with another heavy clunk, and Jean held her breath in anticipation. She exhaled sharply as the door smoothly slid open.

In the center of the room, crouched down on the floor, was a being that looked like a jellyfish, or a cuttlefish, trying to assume the form of a human. His skin was pale and silky and shimmered with a dull sea-green translucence. In the right lighting, his long and thin limbs could be mistaken for tentacles. His elongated frog-like hands were bound in front of him, and the tight cuffs binding them were chained to a link embedded in the concrete floor of the cell. A black cloth bag covered his head, and Jean felt an overwhelming urge to yank it off. She wanted to see his face, no matter how different it might be.

"Azon?" she called out, her voice shaking. She thought she saw the black bag shift in her direction. Her heartbeat racing, Jean moved to enter the room, but the door slid shut before she could. The force was so intense that it knocked her off balance.

Jean was suddenly aware of several heavily booted footsteps rapidly approaching their group. The four of them turned around to find themselves surrounded on both sides of the passageway by a mix of Genesis Sector agents and military-looking troops.

Of course, it was a trap. It had to be. The doctor must have tipped someone off somehow. Perhaps opening the door triggered an alarm? I knew this was way too easy. Urgh! And we walked right into it!

A voice she never wanted to hear again yanked Jean out of her thoughts.

"Miss Anderson, it is *so* good to see you again. I hope you'll be more cooperative this time."

The dark rectangular sunglasses. The impeccably parted hair. The thin line of a mouth. And the golden scythe tie pin, the only glint of color on a harsh black and white suit. It was Agent Smyte, standing at the head of the group of agents blocking them from the way they'd come in.

A lump of thread formed in Jean's throat. They were trapped, several floors and innumerable feet underground, in a top secret government facility that was more than capable of making them disappear without a trace. She had reached the lowest pits of Hell, just as Dante had in *Inferno*.

"You led them right into our hands with minimal trouble. I knew I could count on you to deliver, as always."

Jean thought Agent Smyte was addressing Dr. Gravin. But he wasn't.

"Well done ... Agent Daniels. Well done," Agent Smyte said, clapping his hands.

Jean gasped as her eyes widened. "Kale?"

18

Organization Rules

Two days after completing her tests for the organization, Emmie was asleep in her dorm room when there was a knock at the door. She groggily peeled open her eyes. The knocking continued. She glanced at her phone. It was 1:30 a.m. Carmen was sound asleep, so Emmie trudged to the door while rubbing her eyes. She leaned in and pressed her eye against the peephole and gasped. Dr. Krenik stood on the other side smiling and holding a medium-sized brown box. Emmie yawned and cracked open the door.

"Good morning, Emmie. I apologize for waking you, but I wanted to welcome you to the Starlight Organization. Here's your welcome gift," Dr. Krenik whispered, handing the box to Emmie. "The box also contains your cohort and training information. Have a good day."

"Really? Thank you!" Emmie said, yawning. After shutting the door, Emmie carried the box to her desk and flicked on her desk lamp. Hoping to not disturb Carmen, she gently pulled the tape off the box and opened it. Inside, there was a sleek black tablet with the organization's logo emblazoned on it. She picked it up, admiring its smooth surface, and pressed the power button. A message popped up on the screen. "Emmie, congratulations on passing your tests and joining our organization. This tablet contains information you will need for your training sessions and provides a direct connection to your superiors. Your first assignment is to meet your cohort at the designated location on Saturday morning at 8:00 a.m. Best of luck, Dr. Krenik."

Emmie glanced over her shoulder at Carmen and set the tablet on her desk. She looked in the box and found a black folder with directions, supplies, a logo T-shirt, and a name tag. As Emmie removed the supplies from the box, there was a small notecard at the bottom of the box. She picked it up. Her name was on the front in scratchy handwriting. Emmie unfolded the note with trembling hands. *They have Jean. Don't trust anyone. We're working on getting her back.*

Emmie's chest tightened. *What? Who has Jean?* Suddenly, bright sparks shot off the note. She grabbed the note by a corner, ran to the bathroom, and flushed it down the toilet. She stood in the bathroom listening for any signs of an explosion, but heard nothing.

Emmie perused the tablet's contents to see if there was information about Jean. The tablet contained details about her cohort, training agendas, and seminar material. None of the information mentioned Jean. After a couple of hours, Emmie fell asleep at her desk. Later that morning, she heard a camera click and awoke to find Carmen rummaging through the box. "What are you doing?"

Carmen held her cellphone over the box in one hand as she picked up an item with the other hand.

Emmie grabbed Carmen's wrist. "You're takin' pictures of my stuff?"

"What's the big deal? I saw the box and was curious," Carmen scoffed as she pulled her arm away from Emmie's grip.

Emmie snatched the box out of Carmen's hands. "That's confidential information!"

Carmen rolled her eyes. "Relax, it's not like I'm going to steal any of it. I'm not a thief."

"Well, it's from that organization we applied for. They accepted me and I have to keep everything confidential."

Carmen sighed. "I know. I signed a confidentiality agreement, too."

"Yeah, but they didn't accept you, so I can't share any information."

"They're just supplies. So, when's your first training session?" Carmen asked, a biting edge to her tone.

"Early Saturday morning."

Carmen scoffed. "They're not trying to waste any time, are they? The whole thing seems ridiculous."

Emmie glanced at Carmen as her blood boiled. "What's your problem? It's not my fault you didn't get in."

"I just think it's stupid, that's all," Carmen huffed, fists clenched at her sides. "We both did the same interviews and tests. How am I not good enough, but you are?"

"I don't know. Maybe they knew I would be more dedicated than you."

Carmen let out a harsh laugh. "Yeah, I'm sure your parents' government connections had nothing to do with it."

Emmie could feel her face getting hotter. "I gave a great interview and earned this on my own merits."

"Yeah, right," Carmen snorted. "Well, don't come crying to me when they take up all of your weekends and work you to death." Carmen stormed off to the bathroom and slammed the door shut.

19

Family Confrontation

"Kale?" Jean turned to look at him, but her half-brother was already walking away from their group, calmly joining the agents next to Agent Smyte. Kale turned around and glared back at her, his hazel eyes suddenly cold.

"Kale, what is he talking about?" Jean asked, but he didn't reply. Dr. Gravin scuttled into position next to him. "Kale, please, tell me!" She hadn't minded his characteristic silence before, but now it stung her nearly as much as his betrayal did.

"Agents, restrain our two guests," instructed Agent Smyte, "and keep your weapons trained on them. That young man can be a handful if you give him an inch."

Jamal stepped forward. "What, are you still sore because I beat your sorry—oof!" A soldier gut punched Jamal, forcing him to his knees.

"Kale," Jean's voice trembled as she called out, her eyes darting around the room, "what the heck is wrong with you?" She strained against the unyielding grip of the muscular hands, pressing her forcefully onto her knees. The musty smell of dampness filled the air, mingling with the acrid scent of fear. "These people, *his* people, captured and imprisoned our father! You saw him suffering in that cell right there! They've been hunting us ever since we were born! Why are you doing this?"

"Ah, have you forgotten what I told you, Miss Anderson?" said the doctor, his voice no longer weary. "We only searched for you. We never 'hunted' Kale because we never wanted him. His genetic makeup is flawed, subpar, like all the specimens we produced before the embryos in your group. Kale and the other rejects can never reach your level of aptitude and abilities."

"I've had enough of you," grumbled Kale. "I'm regretting giving you the rest of the antidote."

"After all the torture you've put me through. Who knows what type of permanent damage you caused? I feel like I'm going to pass out any minute." Dr. Gravin turned toward Agent Smyte. "You should have told me this man was working for you. It would have saved us so much unpleasantness!"

"With the way you both get along like a house on fire, I doubt it," said Agent Smyte. "No, I always intended the two of you to be different ways to net the same prize. And I think it's safe to say the results speak for themselves."

Jean attempted to stand, but the men holding her down were too strong. "Kale, you disgust me. I can't believe you betrayed me like this," she spat, her voice shaking. "You're my brother!"

Agent Smyte smirked. "Once the army rejected Kale, leaving him disillusioned and drifting, we didn't hesitate to hire him. Even with suboptimal levels of Sepid DNA, he was a useful asset for us. And he still is."

Jean's eyes were like daggers as she processed Kale's betrayal. "You *knew*. You knew who our father was, where he was, this whole time and—"

"Of course, he knew," interrupted Agent Smyte. "He was a key operative in the mission that led to the Sepid Azon's capture by Genesis Sector five years ago. Kale was the one who led your father into our trap, just as he did you."

"Why, Kale? He's your own blood." Tears stung Jean's eyes and she stubbornly blinked them away. *This is not the time to cry.*

"It's because of his blood, actually. Or, to be more specific, his DNA." Agent Smyte was gloating, without restraint. "Azon is apparently a leading figure in the Sepid colony that came to Earth. His family line contains some of the purest and most powerful genes of their kind and is highly sought after for the Genesis Sector studies and development. We had his DNA on file from a previous encounter. In fact, that's how we determined its immense value. But without the source, our supply was limited. Of course, Azon is impossible to catch when he doesn't want to be found."

"So you used Kale to get to him?"

"Used?" Agent Smyte spewed an ugly bark of a laugh. "Kale practically volunteered! Unlike Azon, we always knew where Kale was. We actively surveilled him ever since he was born at one of our facilities. When Kale took the DNA test for his entrance into the army, I was notified at once. And I suspected that Azon might have been too, given their genetic connection. So I approached Kale shortly after his rejection by the army and told him that his birth father would try to contact him. Kale was *so* bitter and angry about the rejection, and he blamed his father's genes for his failure. It wasn't difficult for me to recruit Kale to our cause and to convince him to set a trap for your father. We have held Azon captive in that cell with us ever since."

Agent Smyte continued, "Whew, all that was a mouthful! Does anyone have a spare bottle of water?" He casually took a canteen from a soldier and gulped from it, blatantly ignoring the tense atmosphere in the passage. When he was done, he wiped his mouth on his sleeve with relish. "Okay, enough with the exposition. Kale, escort that young man to his cell, would you? I would like a word with Miss Anderson."

Kale nodded bluntly and avoided Jean's glare as he grabbed Jamal by the arm and led him away with a few of the soldiers following closely behind. Jean expected Jamal to say something, to fight his way out of the clutches like he did when they first met, but he didn't even put up a struggle. *Jamal's just letting them take him away?* She choked back a sob, frowning at the retreating figures. *Ugh, this is all my fault.* Jean lifted her shirt collar up to her eyes, wiping the flowing tears away.

Most of the other agents and soldiers dispersed as well. Soon, Jean was alone with Agent Smyte and the guards who were restraining her. The dark passageway was utterly suffocating with its bleakness.

Agent Smyte walked closer to her, the echoes of his footsteps feeling like small stabs at her body. He crouched down in front of her and tilted her face toward his with a cold finger.

"I can tell it's been a long day for you, so we'll let you get some rest. We have an extensive to-do list on our hands to go through tomorrow for your testing, and you're going to need every ounce of your alien-hybrid strength for it."

Jean scrunched her brows. "What are you going to do to me?"

He brushed a lock of her brown hair away from her face, then jerked his hand back when she snapped at it with her teeth. Dismissing her attack with a laugh, he said, "Still feisty, are we? Not bad. And as for tomorrow's plans, well, why would I ruin all the fun by telling you what they are?" He stood up with a wicked grin on his pencil line of a mouth and gestured to the guards. "You can take her away now."

Unlike Jamal, Jean wriggled and struggled as hard as she could to release the guards' grip. She screamed every curse her frenzied mind could think of at Agent Smyte's retreating back while the guards dragged her down the passageway. Once Smyte was out of sight past the thick steel entrance door, she continued screaming at the guards. "Where are you taking me?! Let me go! What are you going to do to me!" They were about as responsive to her struggles as the dark concrete floor.

The guards didn't drag her for long. After a few minutes, they roughly shoved her into another nearby cell along the passageway. As Jean stumbled to the ground, she heard a familiar voice. "Jean! Hey, are you alright?"

Jean turned around. Jamal's blue eyes rolled as the agent at the door fired a taser at him. He shuddered and contorted, a faint smell of burned cloth coming from him, before he collapsed on the hard floor with a thud.

"Jamal!" Jean rushed to Jamal's side and waited for the small tremors still rippling through him to stop before turning him over. She anxiously pressed an ear to his chest and exhaled in relief when she heard his heart beating. She turned toward the door. "You animals! How could you—"

CLANK. The door slid shut with a heavy finality, and the dark passageway outside disappeared from view. With a small grunt, she pulled Jamal's body toward the nearest wall and propped him up against it. Knowing that it might be futile, she then went to the door and banged her fists against it anyway. She tried to bang out all her frustration and pain, but the door was as unresponsive as the guards who had thrown her into that cell. Allowing the tears to release from her eyes, she returned to Jamal.

"Are you okay? Why didn't you fight back? You fought all of those men before. What happened?"

Jamal didn't respond, even when she shook him. Beads of sweat clung to his forehead. Jean gently wiped them off with her palm. With a ragged sigh, she left him there and scooted over to the opposite wall of the cell. She leaned against it, hugged her knees, and curled up into a ball. The tears flowed freely, and she let them, wishing they could take the hopelessness out of her as they fell.

What's going to happen to us now? What are those "fun plans" Agent Smyte has in store for me? What am I going to do?

She let out another cry of frustration.

Can anyone get us out of this place? No, because nobody knows we're here. No one except... A familiar face swam into view of her mental eye. Brown hair cropped short like they did in the army, cold hazel eyes, angular features a bit like her own. *Kale.*

"Why, Kale?" Jean asked out loud to nobody in particular. "How could you betray us like this? Remember, being alone in foster care with no mother or father? I know what that was like. We have so much in common. I thought you enjoyed having a sister. Did you ever have any actual feelings toward me or was it all one big lie?"

There was no response. With Jamal still out cold, Jean buried her face in her crossed arms. She couldn't stop thinking about Kale's betrayal.

20

DNA Connections

When Jamal regained consciousness, Jean was still in the same curled up position, wallowing in her distress on the opposite side of their cell.

"Jean? Ugh, that taser really did a number on me. Hey, are you okay?" Ignoring the lingering fogginess from the taser blast, Jamal crawled over to Jean's side of the dingy cell. "Hey, c'mere," he murmured, gently wrapping an arm around her shoulders. Jean tensed before allowing herself to uncurl against him. Her curly hair brushed along his jawline as she settled her head against his chest.

"I promise, no one is going to lay a hand on you, Jean. At least not if I can help it. We're getting out of here. Both of us. I just need you to trust me. Can you do that?"

Jean nodded almost imperceptibly against his shoulder. She leaned into him further, the tension draining from her muscles.

Jamal let out a deep exhale. He had no solid plan yet, but with Jean needing him, he was ready to move heaven and earth to turn his words into reality. For now, he held her close as they took mutual comfort in their embrace. "You okay?"

Jean kept her head lowered. "Let's see, I'm stuck in a cell waiting to be experimented on. What do you think?" The air was stale and metallic on Jean's tongue, hints of mildew and unwashed bodies permeating the enclosed space. She glanced around at the gray walls, dingy and scarred with age. Rough edges of the stone bricks surrounding them grated against her skin whenever she leaned back.

"I'm sorry, Jean. I wish I could have done something."

Jean clicked her tongue and stomped away. "Why didn't you do something? You didn't even try to fight back. You just did what they wanted. And now we're stuck here in a cell for who knows how long."

"Wait, what? Look Jean, I can't kung-fu my way past bullets, you know. And how was I supposed to know that your half-brother would stab us in the back like that? I mean, sure, Kale was all quiet and broody, but I thought he was a decent guy." Jamal trailed off and walked over to the wall near Jean and leaned against it.

"I'm sorry. I'm just so irritated right now," Jean huffed. "I really don't mean to blame you." She sat down with her knees up, wrapping her arms around them.

Jamal slid down, sitting next to Jean. "Look, we'll figure something out, alright? This is a difficult situation, but I've gotten out of way worse messes than this, especially with—look, just, don't give up hope, alright? I promise you, we'll get out of this one too." When that burst of pep talk had absolutely no effect, he banged his head against the wall with another, more frustrated sigh. "God, this is going to suck."

After Jamal's chatter died down, an uncomfortable silence diffused throughout the cell, made even more unbearable by the stark walls and rough floor. Whether there was some kind of soundproofing material in the room, or due to how thick the surrounding walls might have been, no noises of any kind could be heard from outside. The small viewing slot in the door was shut as firmly as the rest of the door.

The room wasn't completely quiet, though. There was a low muttering that resembled a growl emanating from Jean's mouth. She leaned on her side against the wall, muttering to herself, wondering if there had been signs of Kale's true allegiance that she'd missed.

You couldn't have seen this coming, Jean. I wish we could have prepared you. Then this betrayal wouldn't hurt so much. Yes, I understand the pain of being betrayed by your own kin. And that pain is what Kale must have felt as well.

"Why? Because the army kicked him out when they found out he was half-alien? That's not our father's fault! It's not Azon's fault that Kale was an experiment made from his DNA!"

That's not how Kale saw it, I imagine. To him, the army was a desirable place where he might have felt belonging. It was hard to blame them for his misfortune when he still wished to be with them. Far easier to blame the unknown father figure who had nothing he wanted.

"But that's not fair! None of this is fair. If anyone's to blame, it should be the Genesis Sector—wait, who is this? Who are you?" Jean blurted out. She sat upright, widening her eyes in a panic, and looked around the cell. There was nobody else there except for Jamal, who stared at her with his mouth gaping open as if she was something out of a horror movie. *Oh, I must be losing my mind. Now I'm hearing voices.*

It seems this prison has stripped me of my manners. Hello, Jean. I am Azon, your genetic father.

"But ... how? Where are you? I saw you chained up in your cell!"

"Jean? Who are you talking to? I mean, it's a pleasant change from all your growling earlier, but I'm the only one here." Jamal looked as confused as she felt. In the awkward silence that followed, the other voice began speaking.

And I am still in those chains, for the time being.

"But I can hear you, even through all the thick walls in this place!"

Jamal inched closer to Jean. "Hear who? Who can you hear?"

Jean raised her palm in front of Jamal's face. "Wait, Jamal. Let me listen."

It seems that human hearing is not so sensitive to speech that is below a certain frequency. I am communicating with you at one such low frequency, better suited for transmission through several layers of material. Whether you realized it yourself or not, you were speaking to yourself at such a frequency earlier, which is why I assumed I could reach out to you with it.

It then struck her. She *had* been muttering to herself about Kale. She must have switched to an inhumanly low pitch of voice while doing it. No wonder Jamal thought she was growling. She took a deep breath and tried it again. *"You mean something like this?"*

Yes, although it will transmit better if you speak closer to the wall of your cell.

Jean placed her cheek against the wall, and Jamal turned away with a huff. "Great, she's back to growling at the wall now," he said. He stared in bewilderment as she carried on an intense, one-sided conversation. With ... herself? Jamal was confused.

"How did you know it was me? Could you see me from under that hood you were in?"

Not clearly, no. But when you called out to me after the doors to my cell opened, I knew you were of my kin, just like your brother, Kale. Our people have a deep connection to our close family members, which allows us to identify them from a short distance even without visual contact. There are harmonics in the voice that we can pick out to identify our relations—I could find you in a group of over fifty others, even if I had yet to meet you or lay eyes on you.

"And I can do this too?"

"Whoa, wait a minute," Jamal interjected, scooting closer. "Who exactly are you talking to?"

You certainly have the potential for it. But whether you have the ability itself, I cannot confirm.

For the first time in what felt like an eternity, Jean smiled to herself. *"You know, for the longest time, for years, I thought I would never discover who my father was. And now, here we are, talking to each other through concrete walls like it's the most natural thing ever."*

Jean didn't respond to Jamal's question, continuing her cryptic dialogue. Jamal waved a hand in front of her eyes. Nothing. It was like she was in a trance. Unease trickled down Jamal's spine. "Come on, Jean, you're really freaking me out here," he said. "What's going on?" He grasped her shoulder, giving it an urgent shake.

Jean's gaze refocused, drifting over to Jamal. "My father—I can hear Azon talking to me! Leave me alone," she exclaimed breathlessly before launching back into their exchange.

"Woah, woah, slow down!" Jamal interrupted again. "Azon? How are you hearing him? Where is he?"

Jean scooted further away from Jamal. "Jamal, please stop!"

Jamal sat with his mouth gaping open, staring at Jean. "Okay, I'll leave you alone."

It's a special moment for me as well, Jean. For all of us.

"All of us..." Jean remembered the long list of names she saw on her DNA test results sheet. *"There are more like us still here on Earth? How many?"*

Many more, yes. At least 15,000 of us arrived here.

"That many? But we would have noticed so many aliens showing up here at once! Where are the rest of them?"

We are everywhere, I would imagine. Some of us are here in this country, scattered across its area. Others are in places all over your world. Most of my kin—your kin—are near a city called Tucson in a place called Arizona. I would love to introduce you to them one day, our family, should you wish to meet them.

"Our family." Jean repeated it softly to herself a few times. Each time, a light of hope sparked in her eyes, and the cell felt just a bit less hopeless. She didn't just have a father, but a whole family related to her, on Earth. In Arizona, of all places. She couldn't wait to meet them.

"Azon, I saw many artifacts and writings I believe are from our kind, but I couldn't understand what they were saying or showing. Could you ... could you tell me about my heritage? About your, no, our people?"

Of course. Back on Tlatzin, I was a scholar and a teacher. Nothing would give me greater pleasure.

In the brief pause that followed, Jean imagined that Azon was clearing his throat like one of her professors back in Montana. The thought of it brought a welcome chuckle to her lips.

Where to begin? Our people are what we call tlatmolpaii. I think in your language, you would say terraforms. We are beings whose existence, whose livelihoods, whose culture, are based on a strong connection with the land and the sea on which we live, and the natural resources that come from it. Azon's voice swelled with pride as he continued. *From the time of our earliest ancestors, we lived in harmony with our world Tlatzin, taking from it and giving back to it with moderation. The scientists on Earth have a name for this: mutual symbiosis.*

Our people could always change our physical traits to better adapt to the environment we are in. Whether that is because we are tlatmolpaii, or whether we could only be so due to this ability, is something we still debate about. Because of this, our people had an astounding variety of forms and shapes, depending on whether we lived on land or sea, in forests or plains, on mountaintops or underground. Many of us who came to Earth lived in the seas and shallow waters on Tlatzin, which is why we still have something of an aquatic appearance.

"I saw some pictures in the artifacts. They reminded me of pictures we have of the species humans descended from. Were those pictures of your ancestors?"

They could be from our ancestors or from related people who lived in different environments at the same time. As I said, we can vary greatly in form depending on where we live. It was also because of this enhanced adaptability that we could live on Tlatzin for as long as we did. Even when the planet broke, even when it slowly began to die, we still lived on its surface and tried to nurse it back to health. Well, some of us did.

"Your planet ... broke? How? Why?"

There was a long pause. Jean didn't know, but Azon was sighing in sadness at the recollection of the next part of his story.

The trouble started thousands of years ago, but fairly recent within the timeline of our people's existence on Tlatzin. As I said before, we had lived in harmony with our world since the time of our ancestors. We believed that the ideal livelihood was one of coexistence with Tlatzin and its natural resources.

But at some point, a new ideology, or belief system, grew in popularity among our people. Maybe it was because our population had grown too much, or Tlatzin had done something to earn our ire. Whatever it was, the new ideology dictated that Tlatzin was not a neighbor to coexist with, but a thing that we owned, a resource to be exploited and used.

"Subdue the world and have dominion over it."

Something like that. Did you find that in one of our artifacts?

"No, I read it in a book from here, on Earth. So what happened?"

The new ideology took hold among us, and it soon became the dominant one that our people followed. As a result, the old traditions and culture of coexistence were replaced with new ones of harvest and conquest. It was not all bad, I suppose. The more we took from Tlatzin, the more we discovered about it, and the more inventions and technological advancements we made. But in doing so, our numbers grew even larger, and we consumed even more. Year after year, we ate away at Tlatzin's resources without control, without caution. The wisest and most knowledgeable of our kind could foresee that, in time to come, they would be depleted, and our livelihoods would suffer for it.

"Then you could have stopped it, couldn't you? If you knew what was going to happen?"

Sadly, many of us still clung too firmly to the new ideology, to the belief that we were, as you said, in dominion over Tlatzin. We kept warning them, but those with the power and influence to make the necessary changes ignored us or didn't give our warnings the urgency they required. Some believed that the problem would be solved by future generations. Some even discredited us, claiming that we were seeking to misinform everyone in order to cause unwanted destabilization of our society.

"That sounds depressingly familiar."

And during all those years, Tlatzin's core was being depleted further, and its resources were dwindling faster than we could hope to replenish them. The surface of the planet became harsher, less desirable to live on. Without its core at full strength, Tlatzin's magnetic field couldn't shield us from harmful cosmic radiation, and its inner heat could no longer sustain our planet's desired surface temperature. We continued to adapt even as the surface of Tlatzin started to resemble the barren wasteland it would eventually become. And we could see that our efforts were ultimately futile.

"So you had no choice but to leave?"

Indeed. We were advanced enough to build the necessary spacecraft and equipment we needed to evacuate those of us who knew what was coming. We also had technology to find desirable exoplanets that we could travel to within the galaxy. Earth was not the only one our spaceships traveled to.

It was painful, having to say goodbye to Tlatzin, a planet that had hosted us, had nurtured us for so long. It was more painful knowing that we had wronged it so much in return, that it was suffering because of us. But it was our best option for the survival of our people. At least, we like to think so.

Only about half of our people who left for Earth lived long enough to reach it, even though our lifespans extend into centuries. Much of the information I just told you of has been passed down along generations of our people born during the journey and from books and journals we brought with us. And as for Tlatzin ... it must have become an uninhabitable husk by now, a spent shadow of its former self.

Jean let Azon have a moment of silence for his home world.

"So ... why did you choose Earth?"

We had two main reasons. One was that your planet has a large concentration of nitrogen in its atmosphere, which is what we breathe to survive. The other was that your planet had, when we first found it, large bodies of water that were also near sizable stretches of natural vegetation. We lived in similar surroundings back on Tlatzin, so we felt that Earth would be one of the easier planets for us to adapt to. Relatively speaking, of course. We still had to undergo a significant change in our bodies.

"Why? Didn't Earth have everything you needed?"

Earth's gravity is about twice that of Tlatzin's atmosphere. Besides the nitrogen, many other chemicals that make up your natural resources are very different from what we had. Your water is much denser than ours, for instance, and has other altered properties.

"That sounds like a lot to adjust to. How did you manage it?"

The journey here was long enough for those of us in the spacecraft that came here to undergo strenuous simulations that evolved our bodies to be closer to the dominant lifeforms on Earth. To give you an idea of what it entailed, when we left Tlatzin, we were closer in form to the animals you call jellyfish than we were to humans.

"What? But you look so human now! You had to grow a skeleton and everything while in outer space?"

We already had skeletons, but we did have to adjust their shape and strengthen them, yes. Still, the journey being so long had other consequences. According to our information, when we first saw Earth, most of its surface was green, blue, and healthy. When we finally arrived, the land was infested and overrun with constructions of metal and glass, and the waters were turbulent and polluted with chemicals we had not accounted for. And the planet's surface temperature had risen to dangerously high levels, far more than we could have predicted. It made for ... an ominous arrival.

"What happened?"

Sadly, although we arrived on this planet in peace, looking once more for coexistence like our traditions of old, the humans who found us had other ideas. Ever since we landed, your government, as well as others, has gone to great lengths to capture and study us.

Dr. Gravin and other scientists like him have used my DNA, and that of many others of our kind, for experimentation. I believe they hope to merge our species together and by doing so, make humans more resistant and adaptable to the changes to come from humankind's destruction and overconsumption of your planet's resources.

"Right, things like resisting heat and cold and having advanced hearing."

That is just a small taste of your abilities—you are capable of so much more. For instance, were you to find yourself in a sudden cold snap, your body can secrete a layer of cryoprotectant through your blood and around your vital organs that would prevent you from freezing.

"Really? That sounds amazing!"

It is, as I understand the expression, very cool.

Jean groaned. Even alien fathers couldn't resist making dad jokes.

But yes, Dr. Gravin and the other scientists aim to give humans our ability to resist extreme temperatures, our enhanced vision, hearing, and other senses, our camouflaging and regenerative abilities, and many more traits that our kind have.

"Dr. Gravin's work is immoral. You aren't rats to be experimented on."

Certainly, but he is not the greatest concern of mine, and neither should he be of yours. After all, immoral though his work is, he is ultimately driven by the betterment of humankind. Which is a benevolent goal that I can endorse, even if I dislike his methods. No, the bigger threat for us is people like Agent Smyte.

"Agent Smyte? I mean, yeah, that man's a nasty piece of work, but why do you see him as such a threat?"

Agent Smyte wants our DNA, but he doesn't care for the salvation of our species, and he's not doing it for the good of humankind. To him, our genes and our abilities are a weapon to be used in battle. He wants to give his soldiers a tactical advantage in any conflict they might choose to engage in. Humans with advanced senses, able to withstand extreme conditions in the harshest environments on Earth, able even to resist many kinds of physical trauma and injury. Imagine such abilities being deployed in a setting of war.

"He could walk over pretty much anyone who tried to stop him."

Indeed. And from what I can tell, aggressive humans with such power in their hands are the worst kind of threat to humankind, as well as to the rest of the planet.

"And Kale, knowing all this, still helped him?"

I understand your hatred of Kale, but you must also understand, Jean. Before Agent Smyte, your brother was cast aside by society, labeled a freak and worse. I don't know if you had the same experience, but he never recovered from his tormented childhood.

Freak. That word resonated with Jean. It became her nickname after the class trip to the Natural History Museum. Her peers yelled the word whenever she walked down the school hallway and called her the name whenever they addressed her. The class bully spread a rumor that Jean was an abandoned baby because of her freakish nature. Even with the incessant bullying Jean endured during her childhood, she would never turn her back on her family the way Kale did.

And Kale never had a stable family to give him the love and affection he deserved. He bottled up that hurt, that anger inside him, without an outlet, without someone who could relieve it. It was no wonder that when Agent Smyte offered acceptance and friendship, Kale readily took it. And I sense that Kale still doubts the path he has chosen. There is still hope for him.

"You're just saying that because he's your son. I'm amazed you have forgiven him."

Perhaps it's because I know he is a good guy who just needs to find his place in this world. It might also be because I could never stay angry at my own children, no matter what they do. Someday, you will understand.

It felt like they had been talking for ages. Jean was suddenly aware of how tired she was. Not having any means to tell the time, she assumed it was late in the night. She glanced at Jamal who was curled up in the fetal position sound asleep. Rubbing her eyes, she felt a big yawn coming and let it happen. *"Thank you for everything you just told me, Azon. We may be in a hopeless mess right now, but at least I can die knowing more than I thought I ever would about my heritage and my roots."*

I should hope you will not be dying anytime soon, though, Jean.

"But we're all in prison cells, several miles underground, in the middle of nowhere. And Genesis Sector wants to do God knows what to me and you. The future doesn't look great right now."

The future looked bleak to me as well until I discovered that one of my children wants to free me from this place. This has given me added strength of will and a bit more physical strength. You have my thanks for that, Jean, and I promise you, we will find a way to escape.

Those were the last words Jean processed before she closed her eyes and sleep overcame her like a rush of thick fog.

21

War Zone

After an undetermined amount of time passed, the cell's door clicked open. Several guards stepped into the room with Kale following closely behind them. One guard pulled Jean to her feet and dragged her toward the door. She glanced at Kale's smug face. *He should have devil horns perched on his head. They would be perfect for someone with his evil nature.*

Kale pointed at Jamal. "Bring him too."

Two guards grabbed Jamal. With no resistance, Jamal followed the guards out of the cell.

Kale approached Jean and walked next to her. "I'm sorry. I wish you wouldn't have found me and gotten into this mess," Kale whispered into Jean's ear.

"I never would've thought you would betray me like this. We're family." Jean remembered what Azon had told her about forgiveness. If anyone had a reason to not forgive Kale, it would be him. What Kale did to Azon was far worse. *Maybe I can consider forgiving Kale, but no one ever said anything about forgetting what he did.*

"I tried to stop you from coming here."

Jean huffed. "It didn't seem that way to me. I mean, if you had told me they were going to trap me to use for their twisted experiments, I might have thought twice about coming."

Kale fell behind Jean as they entered a laboratory. An intense ammonia smell stung Jean's nostrils. The laboratory was crowded with guards and agents dressed in medical gear standing near Agent Smyte and Dr. Gravin. With a nod, Agent Smyte greeted the guards leading Jean and Jamal. In one corner of the room, a pair of guards restrained a man who appeared to be middle-aged. "Keep Azon there. I'm going to start with the girl first," Agent Smyte said.

Azon turned toward Kale. "Why did you bring her here? You know what they want."

Kale approached Azon. "If you want to see who to blame, look in the mirror."

"Don't make your sister pay for our battles."

"Shut up, old man," Kale huffed.

"I know you blame me for your failures in life, but at least consider me for some of your successes."

Kale turned his back to Azon and marched away. Then he grabbed Jean's arm and helped a guard drag her to a medical bed in the middle of the room. Panic swelled inside Jean and her breath quickened. *I can't believe I was ready to forgive him!* She lifted her legs and attempted to fall to the floor, but Kale's grip was too strong. Jean writhed as the two men strapped her ankles and wrists to the bed.

Dr. Gravin walked over to the bed carrying a large box of syringes and other medical supplies. "Jean, this is your chance to save the world. Your DNA is very important for the advancement of modern medicine."

Jean twisted her body and screamed.

Dr. Gravin motioned to a guard. "Cover her mouth and hold her still." He leaned down toward Jean with his face inches from hers. "Don't worry. We'll sedate you so you won't feel a thing. This won't take long. We're just going to extract samples from your DNA, blood, and bone tissue. We're using it to synthesize a serum. That serum will boost immunity and cure cancers in humans worldwide. And that's just the beginning. We'll be able to do amazing things, thanks to you."

Jean's heart rate increased, and she struggled to breathe against the weight of the guard holding her in place. She took a deep breath and exhaled. Dr. Gravin and his assistants began preparing the tools and equipment to perform the procedures. Suddenly, there was a loud boom just outside of the room.

Agent Smyte peeked out a window on the door. "Proceed, Doctor. Bartow and Thompson, go see what that was." Soon after Bartow and Thompson left, loud gunshots erupted from the hall. Agent Smyte snarled. "We don't have all day, Gravin. Pick up the pace." Agent Smyte dashed across the room and darted out the door.

Dr. Gravin pulled out a syringe and filled it with a clear liquid. Jean glanced at Jamal. He met her terrified gaze and winked. Then he raised his linked arms before spinning around and driving his elbow into the stomach of one of two guards restraining him. The guard doubled over with a loud grunt. Before the second guard could react, Jamal delivered a swift uppercut to his jaw and kneed him in the groin, knocking him to the floor.

Another guard approached. Jamal ducked to avoid a flying bullet from the guard's gun and swept his leg around, kicking the feet from underneath the guard. As the guard plummeted to the concrete floor, Jamal delivered a forceful chop to his neck, rendering him unconscious. Jamal grabbed the guard's gun off the floor.

Two guards rushed toward Jamal. He fired the gun at the guards, striking one in the chest while the other successfully dodged the bullets and continued running forward. Jamal dashed toward the guard, grabbed his outstretched arm, and twisted it, flipping him onto his back.

Jean glanced at Azon standing with a huge grin on his face. When she turned back to look at the doctor, she saw him running toward her with the syringe. Jamal grabbed the doctor by the arm and flung him into the nearest wall, causing the syringe to fly out of his hand and crash onto the floor. The force was so great that the doctor immediately passed out.

Azon's expression changed, and he morphed into the humanoid creature Jean first saw when he was in the cell. He whistled. Azon's eyes met the guards' gazes, and in a mesmerizing display, he defied gravity, effortlessly levitating toward one of them. In a split second, his forehead collided with the guard's nose, causing an audible crunch. As the remaining guards attempted to capture Azon, he dodged and weaved out of their reach with an agility that was beyond any human.

With his hands still restrained behind his back, Azon suddenly leaped into the air, tucked in his legs, and lifted his arms around in a full circle. It looked as if his shoulders had dislocated and realigned without pain or discomfort. With his hands now in front of him, Azon helped Jamal fight and overpower the remaining guards.

During the fight, Kale leaned against a wall, standing with his fists clenched. When Jean looked up at him, he sighed and started handcuffing the knocked-out guards to each other. Jean was relieved. She was happy to see her brother helping Jamal and Azon instead of fighting against them. Suddenly, someone grabbed Jean's arm and stuck a needle into it. Jean turned her head and saw Dr. Gravin standing by her side. "Jamal!" she yelled. Before Jamal could do anything, the laboratory's door burst open and a flood of men and women filled the room. They appeared to be led by an African-American woman who scanned the room and pointed at Dr. Gravin.

Dr. Gravin ran in the opposite direction, but he was unable to get more than a few feet before some of the woman's people captured him and handcuffed his wrists behind his back. The woman continued searching the faces in the room. "Where is he? Where's Smyte?" she asked.

As everyone searched for Agent Smyte, a man rushed into the room. "He's gone."

"What? What do you mean, he's gone?!" the woman yelled.

"He escaped."

"Well, what are you waiting for? Go find him!" she cried. A group of her people hurried out of the room.

Azon appeared beside Jean. She watched as he gently pulled the syringe out of her arm and unfastened her restraints. He helped her off the bed and wrapped his arms around her shoulders. "I greet you, daughter."

Jean smiled and returned the hug. During the embrace, she glanced at her father. His eyes appeared to be a vibrant golden orange, similar to the way her eyes looked at the hotel.

The woman who led the group of people approached Jean.

"Thank you for saving me."

The woman nodded.

Jean sighed. "Um, I'm Jean."

"Yes, I know. I'm Mary Galloway. I'm the lead operative for the Starlight Organization. We fight against anti-Xeno practices, such as those of the Genesis Sector."

Jean nodded as she listened, but grogginess from whatever was in the syringe overtook her. "Wait ... what did you say your name was?"

"Mary Galloway."

"Oh, why does that name sound familiar?" Jean lowered her head toward the ground and tried to gather her thoughts. "My mother." Jean glanced up at Mary. "My biological mother's name is Mary Galloway."

Mary smiled. "That's right, Jean. I'm your mother."

22

Mary's Journey

With every mile down the lonely highway leading her farther away from her baby girl, war raged violently inside Mary's soul. All her hopes and dreams for motherhood battered relentlessly against her terrifying reality. Every time she passed an exit, the urge to turn the car around screamed within her weary mind. *I spent so much time and money on having a baby. How could I abandon her? Did I really have no choice? Were there other options? What if I left the country? I don't know. Maybe this is the best option for now. Ugh, I'm so tired. I can't even think straight. I can't go home yet. This is what's best. Right. This is what's best for now.*

Tears returned, flowing down Mary's cheek. Her heart shattered anew with each passing mile between them. Minutes later, a weathered wooden sign for a campground came into view. As she pulled into the campground, sobs shaking her frame, the decision sat like a boulder in her chest.

She parked in a gravel lot next to a few other cars. The dense forest surrounded her, tall pines and leafy oaks swaying gently in the night breeze. A bird's evening song warbled through the trees. Breathing in deeply, Mary rolled down the windows, inviting the invigorating aroma of pine and campfire smoke into the car. She reclined her seat back, the tension in her muscles uncoiling against the support. Her eyes drifted shut to the natural lullaby of rustling leaves and chirping crickets. As she surrendered to sleep, the vivid sparkle of stars danced across her closed eyelids.

When Mary woke up several hours later, she dialed Caroline's number.

An empathetic voice answered the call. "Hi Mary, how are you?"

"Well, I've been better," Mary said, staring absently out the window.

"I'm so sorry. I wish there weren't such cruel people in this world."

Mary sighed. "Yeah. Well, I'm just glad you let me know Gravin's plans before it was too late. I shudder to think what he would have done if he had gotten his hands on my baby."

"Did everything work out okay with the social worker?"

"Yeah, I dropped her off yesterday."

"Great! I'm meeting with my friend Jaron in a few days and it would be great if you could come too. I met him through my advocacy network and he's been working for Xeno rights for 10 years by helping them get jobs and housing. His wife, Nelia, is originally from Tlatzin."

"What's the meeting about?"

"He's expanding his advocacy program. I don't have details yet, but I'm sure he'll go over everything at the meeting."

"Oh, okay. Do you know when they'll provide an update about Jean? I'm sorry. I don't mean to change the subject, but I just can't stop thinking about her."

"I'll call today for an update."

Mary dabbed her final tear in the corner of her eye with a tissue. "Thanks. I'm not sure about the meeting, but text me the information." As the call ended, the last glowing embers of a nearby campfire dwindled. The family that had tended it for hours wandered off to bed, their laughter drifting through the trees—a reminder of the simple joys she may now never experience with her own child.

Suddenly, hot anger pulsed through Mary's veins. No family should endure this torment. *I won't stop until that doctor pays for what he's doing. I will find a way to expose his experiments and put an end to his medical practice. I don't care how long it takes.*

For all the victims with missing loved ones trapped in a vicious machine beyond their comprehension, Mary knew she had to do something. And for the baby girl whose tiny hand would never hold her own ... she would keep fighting until justice was won. They deserved at least that glimmer of hope.

23

Clearance

After instructing her people to clear out the Genesis Sector base, Mary drove Jean to the Starlight Organization's base several miles away. The orange-dressed sun peeked over an immense concrete structure with few windows. The building's dingy facade let it fade into an industrial area's background. A large electric fence surrounded the building. Small security cameras sat perched on every corner of the building's roof and atop every window.

As they pulled up to the base, Jean grinned. Not only had she met her biological parents, but they were amazing. Her father was a wonderful, caring being who accepted her, even though he had nothing to do with her existence. And her mother spent most of her adult life working to protect other species. What could be better than that? Still, Jean felt awkward sitting next to her biological mother. She called Mrs. Anderson her mom and wasn't sure about the best way to address Mary. Should she call her Mom? Also, Mary didn't seem to have a warm persona like Mrs. Anderson. *I wonder if she's like me and just takes longer to warm up to people.*

After parking the car, Mary stepped outside to speak with some of her men. Jean got out of the car and stood motionless as she was still in shock from everything that happened. A hand rested on her shoulder and she turned around. Azon stood behind her in his human form.

"Jean, you were very brave."

Jean shrugged. "I didn't do anything except try to stay alive."

"Bravery is about more than physically defending yourself. Bravery is about not giving in to fear and doubt."

Mary returned. "There's no sign of Agent Smyte."

Jean scrunched her brows and sighed.

"Don't worry, Jean. We have our best people searching for Smyte. I'm sure we'll find him soon."

Kale inched closer to Mary after reading a message on his phone. "I just received some intel. Smyte's planning an escape in Krenik's boat."

Jamal stepped in front of Kale. "Really, Kale? Why should we believe you? You're the one who led us straight into the lion's den."

"This is not the time to argue with each other. Kale stood with us at the Genesis base and he's on our side now," Azon said.

"That's what's important," Mary said. "Look everyone, anti-Xeno practices are illegal. The U.S. government is after Smyte and Gravin. They became rogue and started their own sub-government organization doing human and Xeno experiments. We believe they're doing it to create a type of superhuman who can help further their goals of achieving world domination. After discovering the experiments, the government ended their employment, but they fled before we could arrest them. Unfortunately, we don't know everyone involved in their organization, and we suspect there are multiple locations around the world."

"Um, Mary. Uh, Mom. Can we speak privately?" Jean asked, her voice trembling.

"Sure." Mary's eyes misted when Jean called her "Mom." She led Jean to a small conference room near the lab. "Do you mind if I give you a hug?"

Jean shook her head and rushed into Mary's arms. Mary held her, tears spilling down her cheeks as she stroked Jean's hair. They held each other tightly for a couple of minutes.

"I'm so sorry," Mary whispered, her body shaking. "You have every right to hate me. The story we planted was so terrible. Please know, I never abandoned you."

"I never hated you. You gave me life, and I knew you did what you felt was best. I have great parents, so things worked out in the end."

Mary pulled back with her eyes fixed on Jean's eyes and clasped her hands. "So, tell me. What would you like to discuss?"

"I guess I have questions about my birth and why I ended up in foster care. My parents said someone found me in a park. I was wondering what happened."

"Well, that's a long story, but I can give you the short version for now." Mary sighed as she wiped a tear from her cheek with the back of her hand. "My original plan wasn't to abandon you in a park. I saw Dr. Gravin as a patient due to fertility issues. A few months after he implanted an embryo in me, one of his former employees contacted me and told me that my husband's sperm was not used to create the embryo. She explained what Dr. Gravin had done and warned me that you were in danger. She said Gravin planned to take you and use you in experiments. Of course, I definitely didn't want that to happen. So after you were born, I had an acquaintance claim to find you in a park. Jean, please know I did what I had to do."

"I understand. I always wondered why you didn't want me."

"There was never a time I didn't want you, but I was happy to see the court approve your adoption when you were thirteen." Mary winked.

"You knew about that?"

"Let's just say sources kept me informed. If I couldn't be in your life, I wanted to at least make sure you were okay. And sometimes I was in the background watching."

"In the background? Wait, I knew you looked familiar. Was that you? I mean, were you at the museum ten years ago?"

Mary chuckled. "You remember! Yes, that was me. I did a little peeking into your life occasionally to make sure you were okay. Sometimes, it was better to see things with my own eyes," she said with a wink.

"What about Dr. Gravin? Didn't he wonder what happened to me?"

Mary grinned. "I told him you were stillborn. I got a fake death certificate and fake medical records through my hospital and government connections. I don't know if he really believed me, but he didn't seem to suspect anything until your DNA test pinged the system."

"I'm starting to regret taking that test."

"Oh, don't say that. We got to meet because you took it. Jean, I spent years working for the government fighting against men like Smyte, Gravin, and the Genesis Sector regime. I kept you safe by keeping an eye on you in the background. After your DNA test came in, I sent Agent Walker to make sure you stayed safe."

Jean scrunched her brows. "Agent Walker?"

'I'll be right back." Mary left the room and returned with Jamal. "This is Agent Walker, but you may know him as Jamal."

"You knew my mother all along? Why..."

Mary's phone buzzed. "I need to take this call. Agent, please show Jean to a room where she can rest for the evening." Mary hurried out of the room.

"I'm sorry. I wanted to tell you. I was aware of Kale's betrayal of Azon, so I couldn't reveal my identity in case he was still loyal to Agent Smyte." Jamal guided Jean to a small room with a bed, desk, and chair. "I'll go pick up some pizza."

Jean sighed. "I still don't understand. I would have kept your secret."

"I'm sorry. It was safer to not know. And if Kale was against your father, there was a chance he would have a problem with you, too. The risk of compromising our entire organization was too great." Jamal gently kissed Jean on the forehead.

Jean scrunched her brows and stepped back.

"Oh, um. I'm sorry." Jamal rubbed his hands together.

"You know, I just thought about something. Mary said something about making sure I was safe. She looks so familiar. I keep thinking I may have seen her before."

"Maybe you have seen her or someone who looks like her. Look, I know you're hungry. I'm gonna go get the pizza," he said before leaving.

While resting in her room, Jean was startled when one section of the wall flickered, becoming a transparent digital window displaying a lush, mountainous landscape. Her eyes grew heavy, as if they had weights pulling them down. She yawned as drowsiness washed over her. Before long, she plopped onto the bed and fell asleep. After a half hour, she heard someone breathing. She peeled her eyes open. Agent Smyte towered over her, his thin lips curled into a sinister smile. Before she could move, he shoved a moist cloth over her face. Suddenly feeling exhausted, Jean was unable to keep her eyelids open, and everything turned to blackness.

24

Blindsided

Jean awakened to discover that Agent Smyte had driven her to an unknown dock with rows of a wide variety of boats. Some were old and others were new. There were also boats of varying sizes. Jean blinked and fought to keep her eyes open. Agent Smyte opened the passenger door and pulled Jean from the car. He forced her forward and led her down a timber ramp toward the water.

Agent Smyte searched the rows of boats with his eyes. "Where's that idiot?" he huffed.

Suddenly, someone whistled. Jean and Agent Smyte turned toward the direction of the sound. Dr. Krenik stood on the deck of an old, shabby tugboat, waving his arms. "What is that? That's all you got?" Agent Smyte yelled.

Jean laughed. "Surely, you don't expect to get far in that thing."

"Shut up," Agent Smyte grunted. He shoved Jean and pulled her forward toward the vessel. They made their way up to the wheelhouse, where Dr. Krenik was attempting to start the engine. After climbing aboard the boat, Agent Smyte approached the doctor. "This is the boat you were talking about? How are we supposed to get anywhere on this?"

"This was all I could get. Nothing else was available on such short notice." Dr. Krenik paced. "It's not like we have access to our old amenities, being government outcasts and all."

Agent Smyte pulled Jean over to the corner beside an old wood heater and Jean winced as coarse rope stung her wrists while the agent tied her up. She wriggled her arms and rubbed her wrists together, trying to become unbound.

"I guess you won't be able to synthesize my DNA now," said Jean, spitting out the words through gritted teeth. Her body tensed, so she took a deep breath to clear her mind. *What can I do? Jamal's not here to help. If I can't escape, I'll end up like Azon, wasting away in a cell for years while experiments are conducted on me.* Jean studied her surroundings. There didn't seem to be much on the boat that she could see besides a small heater and a few life jackets. *I need to come up with a plan. Maybe I can get him to let down his guard if I pretend to surrender.* Jean leaned against the wall and closed her eyes.

"There will always be other doctors to take Gravin's place." Agent Smyte smirked while he tightened the rope around Jean's wrists. Then he sighed. "I need a drink."

"There's something in the cabin below," Dr. Krenik said.

"Well, then that's where I'm going. Watch her." Agent Smyte left through the door and headed down the ladder to the lower cabin.

After Agent Smyte left, Jean opened her eyes and Dr. Krenik returned to working on starting the boat. Finally, the engine roared, and he steered the boat away from the dock, driving it toward the middle of the lake. After the boat seemed to steadily head in the right direction, he sat down and became preoccupied with his cellphone.

Seeing Dr. Krenik distracted, Jean wriggled and tried to twist out of the ropes. Her eyes darted around, seeking anything that could serve as a makeshift tool to sever the restraining ropes. She turned and saw a hot poker sticking out of the heater next to her. *Hmm, I wonder if I can use that to break the rope? I guess it doesn't hurt to try.* Jean slowly raised her wrists so that the rope restraints touched the hot poker. The rope made a sizzling sound, but it failed to loosen. Jean scooted closer to the heater and touched the rope to the hot poker again. After a couple of minutes, the rope ripped apart as it caught on fire. Jean tossed the burning rope onto the floor. She frantically scanned the boat, searching for something to use against Krenik, before her eyes fell on the poker in the heater. Taking a deep breath, Jean touched the poker with her hand. It felt cool to her skin.

With the poker in her outstretched arm, Jean stood and dashed toward Krenik. Dr. Krenik raised his arms, waving them. "Wait, wait! I need to tell you..."

This man must be nuts if he thinks I'm going to talk to him. Jean lunged forward and struck him in the head with the hot poker. He immediately passed out, dropping to the floor. She scurried to the wheel and paused as she pondered how to stop the boat. The sky was pitch black. Jean sighed. In the distance, she saw the outline of the quay wall. She turned the heavy wheel and tied it to the quay with rope from her restraints.

With a sudden burst of energy, Jean sprinted out of the wheelhouse and leaped down the ladder. A light appeared from around the corner. Jean ducked behind a small pile of large boxes and crouched down as Agent Smyte came into view. Jean held her breath as she peeked through an opening between the boxes.

"Krenik! How long will it take to get there? Krenik!" Agent Smyte headed toward the ladder carrying a torch. "Where are you?" Smyte raised his torch and looked around as he placed a foot on the ladder. As he turned, the light brightened Jean's face. He ran toward her.

Jean hopped up and ran from behind the boxes toward the side of the boat.

"Smart move, Jean. Where are you gonna run to?"

"I won't let you get away with what you're doing to my people."

"Your people?" Agent Smyte chuckled. "Your people? You mean those monsters? None of you are people. Cur, that's what you are. You're no better than worthless dogs on the street."

"And what are you doing? Chasing my DNA to strengthen the human race? It sounds like we're not the worthless ones."

Agent Smyte lunged at Jean, dropping the torch near his feet. Jean pushed Smyte to the ground, and they wrestled. The boat swayed violently as Jean grappled with Agent Smyte, their fight carrying them dangerously close to the uncovered fuel line. Neither noticed the escaping hiss of gasoline rapidly pooling across the deck plates beneath their feet. Suddenly, the boat jolted as it collided with the stone wall of the quay, fracturing the fuel line. Highly flammable liquid gushed out in a spreading tide.

Still locked in their struggle, Jean and Smyte tumbled hard against the deck. The torch Smyte had dropped skittered across the ground, coming to rest amidst the growing lake of fuel. Noxious fumes filled the air. Jean stood up and Agent Smyte reached for her leg. A colossal explosion bellowed into being, generating a wall of intense heat and fiery debris as it ripped through the metal hull like paper. The bone-jarring force threw Jean off her feet and flung her into the water like a ragdoll. Within seconds, a wall of fire surrounded her.

25

Transformations

The aroma of hot pizza permeated the air as Jamal hurried down the hall, balancing the large, flat box carefully in his hands. Halfway to Jean's room, he slowed. Was her door open? His pace quickened as unease tickled his spine. Upon entering her empty room, Jamal circled slowly. "Jean?" he called out. His pulse spiked as he strode into the adjoining bathroom. *Where is she?* He tossed the pizza onto the bed and called Mary. "Is Jean with you?"

"What do you mean? I sent her with you."

"I know, but she's not here. I went to grab some pizza. When I came back, she was gone."

"What? You were supposed to keep an eye on her!"

"I know. I just ... I'm sorry. I guess I wasn't thinking."

Mary sighed. "Okay, let me call you back."

Jamal paced up and down the hallway, peeking into various rooms. After five minutes, his phone buzzed. It was Mary calling back. "You find her?" he asked.

"No, but I believe she's with Smyte. I think there's someone from the inside who let him in, so we have to be very careful. Don't tell anyone, but we were able to track his location. He's heading toward the dock."

"Okay, I'm on it." Jamal sprinted through the building and out the back door. He hopped onto the nearest motorbike and sped toward the harbor. As soon as he arrived at the dock, he leaped off the motorbike. He heard a car behind him and turned around. Mary, Azon, and Kale climbed out of a jeep and faced the water. Several other vehicles pulled up and parked near Jamal's motorbike. He turned around and sprinted to the end of the jetty. It was so dark, he could barely see as he gasped for breath. Looking out over the water, he could hear the gentle lapping of waves against the shore, and a sudden chill ran down his spine as he felt someone standing behind him.

Mary tapped Jamal on the shoulder. "Do you see anything?"

"Um, no."

"Over there," Kale yelled as he pointed at the quay's border while standing at the opposite side of the jetty. "I think I see a tugboat."

"Okay, guys, I see an unoccupied dinghy." Mary pulled a pair of binoculars out of her duffel bag. "Let's grab it and ride out to the tugboat. I think I see movement."

After climbing into the dinghy, the group headed toward the tugboat. With every step closer, Jamal's heart pounded louder and faster in his chest. Mary lifted the binoculars to her face and peered through them.

Suddenly, a loud boom echoed through the dark sky as enormous waves shoved the tugboat into the quay, causing it to burst into flames. The sudden jolt of the dinghy sent Jamal plummeting to the floor. He jumped up and squinted as he turned toward the fire. "Jean! Jean, where are you?" Jamal yelled as he stared at the burning tugboat. Mary peered through her binoculars, looking for any sign of life.

After fifteen minutes, Mary sighed. "I think we should head back. I'll have divers and a search crew come out." She turned the boat around and headed toward the dock while Jamal and Azon stood at the back, staring at the flames.

"I'd like to help with the search. I want to do whatever I can," Jamal said.

"Wait, I see something moving in the water." Azon rushed to Mary's side. "Let's go back. Hurry and turn the boat around."

As they approached the burning wreckage, Jamal saw a body floating in the water. He squinted. "Is that her?" He kneeled and leaned over the boat's edge. "I see something that looks like a body."

"I'm going to get as close as I can," Mary said.

As they pulled closer to the body, it appeared to be amoeba-like with a head that seemed to change shape every second and bright eyes that appeared to be a warm orange-yellow color. Slowly, the being's features shifted. Jamal hopped up. "It's Jean! Hurry! Jean's in the water. She's alive." Jamal smiled. "I can't believe it. She's actually alive!" When the boat reached Jean, Jamal leaned over the side and held out his hand to help her up. Jean covered her chest with one arm.

Jean shook her head. "My clothes are gone."

Mary searched the boat and found a blanket under a seat. While Azon, Kale, and Jamal turned their backs to Jean, Mary helped her climb onto the boat and wrapped the blanket around her shoulders.

Jamal watched as Jean looked down at her arm. Her skin shimmered from the aftereffect of her change into her Xeno form.

"Don't tell me you're fireproof," Kale groaned. "Are females the only ones who can do that?"

Azon chuckled. "I wouldn't suggest testing that theory, son."

Jamal looked at Jean as she smiled at her family. Mary turned the boat back toward the dock.

Jean plopped down on a rough weathered bench and exhaled as she stared at the water. "Is Agent Smyte gone?"

Mary's shoulders tensed. "I don't know. If he's out there somewhere, we'll find him. We won't stop until we find him or his body."

"So, I guess I'll just need to keep looking over my shoulder for now." Jean imagined Smyte bursting into her dorm at any moment with a gun aimed directly at her.

Mary sat down next to Jean. "It might be safer for you to wait a while before returning to campus. We have a program where we can give you a new identity and keep you hidden."

"Like the Witness Protection Program?" Jean turned to study Mary's face.

Mary grinned. "In some ways, but better."

"Does that mean I won't be able to see my parents or friends?" Jean cleared her throat. "Uh, I mean my other parents. And college?"

"We have a lot of ways to keep you safe and allow you to visit family and friends. For now, the remote option for college will be best."

"That's a lot to think about."

"I don't mean to sound harsh, but you don't have time to think. Time is of the essence. Either you come with me now or you're on your own. I have a personal interest in keeping you safe, but you're an adult. The decision is yours."

Jean stared at the ground as she pondered the thought of giving up everything she knew in her life. She loved college and had just started getting used to managing the daily grind of college classes and studying. Taking remote classes would be a novel experience. And, although

Jean finally met her biological parents, she still wanted to maintain a relationship with the parents she knew and loved. And what about her roommates? They were her first real friends, and they had no idea what happened to her. Were they worried? Jean sighed. She knew what she had to do, but it would be difficult. "Okay, I'll go," she mumbled.

"Great! Jamal will help get you settled in your life. And don't worry. This is temporary. We have advanced techniques for keeping you safe. Once we get your information removed from databases and memories, you will go back to your normal life."

Jean knitted her brows. "Memories?"

"Let's just say, you'll be wiped from every system that identifies you as anything other than your average human college student."

"But, how..."

Mary grabbed Jean's hand, leading her toward Jamal. "Look, it's safer for you to not know everything. Let's hurry and get you out of here. As I said, time is of the essence."

"Will I get to see you again?"

"Of course." Mary gave Jean a hug. "Until we meet again."

26

New Beginnings

Jean dozed off and on as Jamal drove to their destination. He refused to tell her where they were going. She wondered why there was such a big secret. After all, she did not have her cellphone, so no one could use it to track their location. And she was good at keeping secrets, especially when her safety was involved. After a short nap, Jean opened her eyes and shifted in her seat, trying to get comfortable. Her bladder was full, and she needed to find a restroom soon. She looked out the window and saw nothing but desert. There was no sign of civilization in the bleak and unforgiving landscape.

Jean turned toward Jamal and gently nudged him. "Bathroom," she mumbled.

"Huh? Did you say something?"

Jean yawned. The sun was bright and she pulled down the window shade. "Oh, um, can we make a bathroom stop?"

Jamal chuckled. "Nah, you have to wait until we get there. Only a few more hours."

Jean leaned forward and tightly crossed her legs. "What? I don't think…"

"I'm kidding. There's a truck stop at the next exit. Can you reach in the back and grab the tote on the floor?"

Jean rotated toward the back seat and grabbed the tote off the floor. "Here."

"Oh, that's for you. There are wigs and other things you can use to conceal your identity."

Jean scrunched her brows. "You always keep these in your car?"

"Well, they're tools in my line of work. If you don't see anything you like, don't worry. There will be more options where we're going. Just pick something to use for now."

Jean sifted through the items in the bag. "You wear these things? What type of shady stuff are you involved in?" Jean giggled as she imagined Jamal wearing a short blonde wig cut in a bob and large sunglasses.

"Remember? I could tell you. But then, I'd have to kill you."

Jean gasped. *I don't know what to believe anymore. He pretended to not know about my Xeno DNA and he knew my mother the entire time. How am I supposed to know when he's telling the truth?*

Jamal winked. "I'm kidding. Look, there's a lot we'll discuss later. But first, let's focus on the bathroom break and grabbing a bite to eat."

"I've never even worn a wig," Jean said as she haphazardly slipped the wig onto the top of her head. Her long curls flowed under the wig and were still visible. "How's this?"

Jamal laughed and gently tugged a ringlet dangling under the wig. "Ah, no. I think it would be easier to just pin your hair up for now. Slip on the cap and sunglasses and we'll be good to go."

⁂

After driving a few more hours, Jamal exited the freeway and passed a sign that read *Carlin, Population 3000.* They drove down a long two-lane road before turning into a long, winding driveway.

"Welcome home," Jamal said as he stopped in front of a small home. "This is where we'll stay until it's safe for you to return home."

"It's like there's nothing here. I've never lived in such a small town." Jean rolled down her window and glanced at the home. It differed from what she expected while driving down a long, narrow road along a barren landscape. The home resembled a log cabin and it was surrounded by a variety of succulents. It seemed as if the home belonged in a forested area instead of a desert.

Jamal unlocked his vehicle. "It's cool here. Everyone looks out for one another and they're all allies."

"Allies?"

"Yeah, they're either part of our organization or they're a friend or family member of someone who is." Jamal began unloading boxes of supplies from his trunk.

A dog barked incessantly. A woman wearing an enormous cowboy hat with a bright smile stepped out the front door with a large barking dog following closely behind. She walked toward Jamal and Jean. The dog ran up to Jamal and stopped barking. Jamal reached down and hugged the dog. "He's happy to see ya. It's been a long time," the woman said.

"Annie, this is Jean. She's going to stay here awhile."

"Howdy, Jean," Annie said as she tipped her cowboy hat.

"Hello."

"Come on, let me give you the grand tour. We'll get you some rest before you begin training."

"Training?" Jean imagined herself in a gym with Jamal training her in the art of kung fu. Surely, it would take a long time to develop his skills.

"Oh yeah, Jean," Jamal said, rubbing his fingers through the top of his hair. "There are some things we still need to discuss. Let's get settled and we'll talk about everything later."

The three of them entered the small home, which was cozy and had a certain charm. The scent of fried chicken filled the air. Jamal brought various boxes into the home while Annie showed Jean around. As Annie conducted the tour, Jean couldn't help noticing a large cabinet filled with various weapons. There were swords, knives, guns, and some high-tech items Jean could not identify. This was not how she expected to spend her first year in college, but she knew she had to trust Jamal and her biological mother. After the tour, Annie showed Jean to her room. It was a small but comfortable suite with a twin bed and a small dresser. There was also a small bathroom adjoining the room. In some ways, it reminded Jean of her dorm room.

"Make yourself at home, honey. Dinner will be ready soon. Oh, and there are some clothes in the closet. Take whatever you need."

"Thank you."

"You're welcome, sweetie. Let me know if there's anything you need to make you more comfortable," Annie said before she left and closed the door.

Jean plopped onto the bed and let out a deep sigh. She couldn't believe she was in the middle of nowhere with a man she barely knew. But then again, she had no choice.

After dinner, Jamal led Jean to the living room. "I have a surprise." He left the room and returned with a projector.

"Oh, is my training starting already?" Jean asked.

Jamal chuckled. "I know you're anxious to get started, but this is even better." Jamal finished setting up the projector and turned it on. "I know you haven't had a chance to speak to your adoptive parents, so here they are."

The projector shimmered as a hologram of Mrs. Anderson appeared. She had tears in her eyes as she glanced at Jean, but she quickly replaced them with a broad smile. "I'm so glad you're safe," she said, her voice trembling slightly. "We were so worried about you. I kept calling and calling and couldn't reach you."

"I was worried about you, too. Did you get my messages?"

Mrs. Anderson shook her head. "Something's wrong with my voicemail. I don't get a lot of my messages."

Jean flashed a huge grin. "Well, this is much better than talking on the phone. It's like you're standing here in front of me."

Mr. Anderson appeared in the projection. "Hi, sweetheart, how are you?"

"Dad! Hi, I'm good. I miss you."

"I miss you, too," Mr. Anderson said.

"So, what do you know? How did you find out where I was? Or, do you know where I am? Do you know about everything that happened?"

"Well, a nice lady stopped by and said she was your biological mother. She said her colleague was with you to keep you safe," Mr. Anderson said.

"She also had us stay at her company's facility near the university for a couple of days, so she could make sure we weren't in danger. Also, she promised she would arrange for us to see you." A wide smile spread across Mrs. Anderson's face. "Your bio mom was very nice, and she has your smile. I can definitely see a family resemblance."

Jean turned toward Jamal and mouthed "thank you" with a smile. "I'm so happy to see both of you." Jean hopped up and attempted to hug her mother's holographic image. After waving her arms into empty air, she giggled. "Oops, this seems so real. I forgot you aren't really here."

The Andersons chuckled and Mrs. Anderson blew a few kisses in the air to Jean. Jean returned the air kisses and sat down.

"Jean, do you know what all of this is about? Why does your other mother need to keep you safe? She wouldn't give us much information," Mr. Anderson asked.

Jean paused and glanced at Jamal. "I'm not sure how much I'm allowed to say." Jamal nodded. "Well, my biological father has some unique traits. He's actually from another planet. There are people who want to do experiments on people like me."

Mrs. Anderson grinned. "I always knew you were wonderfully special, Jean. I'm glad your Mom #2 is keeping you safe."

Mr. Anderson nodded his head. "Yeah, she seems up to the task with those big guns. There used to be a guy in my bowling league who said he was an alien. That was about twenty years ago. Of course, no one believed him."

Jean giggled. "Well, now you know he might have been telling the truth."

Mr. Anderson chuckled. "I wonder whatever happened to that guy. Maybe I'll look him up."

"Jean, did they say when you can come home?" Mrs. Anderson asked.

"Not yet."

"We hope to get Jean back to her normal life by the end of the semester," Jamal said.

Jean gestured toward Jamal. "Oh, I'm so sorry. Mom, Dad, this is Jamal. He's the one who's been helping me."

"Nice to meet you, Jamal. Jean's lucky to have you in her corner," Mrs. Anderson said.

Mr. Anderson yawned. "It's great seeing you, but I don't know how much longer I can keep my eyes open."

"Okay, I guess I'll let you go and get some sleep as long as Jamal promises I can talk to you like this again."

Jamal grabbed the bag used to store the projector and pulled it closer. "Not a problem. I can set this up for you as often as you want."

"Okay, bye Mom and Dad. I love you." Jean and her parents exchanged air kisses.

After Jean and her parents said their goodbyes, Jamal packed up the projector.

Jean sighed. "So, what now? What type of training was Annie talking about?"

"Well, before we send you back, we want to make sure you at least have some basic self-defense skills. Also, people with Xeno DNA have special skills. We want to make sure you can use your skills to your advantage."

"At Genesis, my father taught me a little about how we can communicate without being in the same room. What other special skills do I have?" "I'm not completely sure. Everyone with partial Xeno DNA has different strengths. Later this week, you will spend a couple of days with a family that has 100% Xeno DNA. They will work with you to help you strengthen your Xeno abilities."

Jean grinned. "Sounds cool."

"Yes, it really is cool, just like you."

"Thanks." Jean stared at the floor as she thought about how her life had changed in a few short days. Although she looked forward to learning more about herself, she felt like a foster kid again, traveling to new places and sleeping in strangers' homes.

Jamal's forehead creased with worry. "What's wrong?"

"Nothing. I was just getting used to college and everything has changed."

"Don't worry. You'll be able to return to college and I'm sure we'll catch Smyte. And now you know your biological parents. Things can only get better from here."

"I sure hope you're right. So, tell me. How did this start for you?"

"What do you mean?"

"How did you start working with Ma—my biological mother?"

"Well, my best friend and roommate in college, Akor, was Xeno. I didn't know it at first. He seemed like a normal guy, but someone discovered his true identity during our last year of college and attacked him. When that happened, I was shocked because Akor was a popular guy with a lot of friends and no enemies. Everyone loved him. I was trying to get him to go to the hospital when showed me his actual appearance and explained why the attack happened. I couldn't believe what I was hearing."

"How can people be so cruel?"

Jamal shrugged. "No idea. Akor's parents brought him to Earth at a very young age and no one had attacked him before. After that happened, his father told me about the company that protected Xeno from the hatred and violence directed toward them simply because they were different. They were hiring, and I applied for the job. I had to go through an intense and rigorous training program that included various forms of martial arts and..."

Jean's eyes grew heavier as she tried to stifle a yawn. "One thing's for sure, you're a great actor. I really believed you didn't know I was an alien," Jean said groggily as she closed her eyes.

"Am I keeping you awake? It's only eight-thirty."

"No. Hmm, maybe." Jean yawned. "Yeah, I think I might be ready for sleep."

"I thought you were going to stay up all night with all that sleeping you did on the way here."

"Ha, ha, ha."

Jamal chuckled. "Well, I guess it's good for you to get plenty of rest. We have an early start tomorrow."

Jean blinked open her eyes. "Why so early?"

"We have a lot to do in a short amount of time. You want to get back to school as soon as possible, don't you?"

"Uh, yeah. Well, goodnight." Jean got up and strolled to bed.

27

Training Day

The next morning, Annie cooked a hearty breakfast of eggs, bacon, and waffles. After breakfast, Jamal led Jean to a large shed behind the house. Inside the shed, there was a large punching bag, floor to ceiling mirrors along one wall, a treadmill, several yoga mats, and weights. A water cooler with paper cups perched nearby sat in the room's corner.

"First, we'll start with some beginner martial arts training. Then, I'm going to go do an introduction to computer and network security."

"Is all of this really necessary? I mean, I'm just going to return to college and be a regular student, aren't I?"

"Well, yes, and no. Most people will see you as a regular college student, but there will always be people looking for people like you. Smyte wasn't working alone and we still haven't found him."

"So, I will be able to fight off a group of people like you took down those men?"

"Honestly, Jean, I'm not sure. But I'd be willing to bet that you'd be able to do it with far less training than the average human."

"Okay, then. I'm ready!" Jean had never done martial arts before, but she was willing to learn. The discipline and focus required to master martial arts fascinated her. She slipped off her shoes and followed Jamal to the center of the room. Jamal started by showing her basic kicks and punches. He also showed her how to position her body and balance her weight evenly between her feet for improved stability.

"Now, let's try a combination." Jamal performed a sequence of moves involving a kick, punch, and a block. Jean watched closely and tried to imitate him. At first, she stumbled each time she tried the combination, but she soon could do it perfectly.

"Great job. Now, let's try something a bit more advanced." Jamal showed Jean a more complex sequence of moves that involved several kicks, spins, and jumps.

Jean stared in amazement as Jamal executed the moves with grace and precision. When it was her turn to try, a surge of excitement and adrenaline mixed with uncertainty flowed through her veins. "Hmm ... I'm not sure about that one," she said, pursing her lips.

"You've got this. Follow along with me." Jamal guided Jean through the sequence step by step while she copied his moves.

With each practice, Jean's confidence grew. Her body became stronger and her movements more agile.

After practicing the sequence together several times, Jamal leaned against the nearest wall. "Okay, now try it by yourself."

Jean strutted to the center of the room and completed the sequence, executing it almost flawlessly.

Jamal beamed as he ran over to Jean and high-fived her. "See, I knew you could do it. You're a natural."

Jean grinned as a sense of pride and accomplishment washed over her. She had never been athletic or coordinated in the past, and she had mastered complex martial arts moves within a few hours. Perhaps her father's DNA was starting to really kick in. She grabbed some water from the water cooler and gulped it down.

"Okay, let's do some stretching to cool down before lunch," Jamal said, drenched in sweat. He grabbed a towel and wiped sweat from his forehead before grabbing a couple of yoga mats and placing them in the center of the room.

Jean peeked at herself in the mirror. She didn't have nearly as much sweat as Jamal and her body temperature was stable. Throughout her life, others often talked about how hot they were after working out and she tended to wonder why she didn't feel the same way. After speaking with Azon, it now made sense. Her body was adjusting its temperature as needed.

Jamal led Jean through a variety of yoga stretches on the mat. Whenever Jamal touched Jean to correct her form, a gentle jolt of electricity shot through her body. "Relax deeply into the stretch. Inhale through your nose and exhale through your mouth," Jamal said every time he showed her a new stretch.

After stretching, they headed to the house for lunch. "Jamal, is there any chance I can speak to my roommates today? Also, I need you to get their phone numbers for me."

"I'm sure I can arrange a call through a secure line. I'll have Annie see if she can find their number online. I can't promise we'll be able to make it happen today, but I'm sure we can make it happen sometime this week."

Jean grinned from ear to ear. "Thanks so much!"

After lunch, Jamal led Jean to a small office next to the kitchen. He set her up with an account on the Starlight Organization's private network and showed her how to communicate with its members. "Your biological parents have an account on this system so you can send messages directly to them. I'm also going to add you to a private group for people who have both human and Xeno DNA. This network is completely internal. You can't use it to access public websites or external email accounts. There's no connection to the regular internet you use and you can't use Wi-Fi to access it."

"So, I won't be able to access the system when I return to school?"

"We can set it up for you at school. You will only be able to access the system using a special tablet we'll provide. You won't be able to use your personal computer."

"Well, I'm glad I'll have a safe way to contact my bio parents."

"Now, let me show you how to hack into a security system," Jamal said, grinning mischievously.

Jean's eyes widened in surprise. "Is that even legal?" she asked, a hint of nervousness in her voice.

Jamal chuckled. "Relax. I wouldn't teach you anything that would get you in trouble. This is just for educational purposes. We're using a network that's strictly for training. It's not real."

"Okay, but I'm not sure I'll ever need that information," Jean said, giggling. She logged into the secure network, eager to message her biological parents. But as soon as she connected, red warning lights flashed on the monitor.

"We've got a security breach!" Jamal shouted, frantically typing commands. "Someone's trying to hack into the system."

Jean's pulse spiked. "What should we do?"

"I'm going to isolate the intrusion point and shut down their access before they penetrate our firewall."

Jamal's nimble fingers danced across the keyboard, a symphony of *clicks* and *clacks* echoing through the room. But before they could stop the attack, hackers assaulted a second section of the network.

The relentless hackers unleashed their onslaught, striking from every angle, like a swarm of relentless bees. Jamal and Jean kept their eyes fixed on the glowing screen as Jamal entered code after code, sweat trickling down their temples.

With each passing minute, the weight of exhaustion settled upon Jean's shoulders, but her determination was unwavering. The battle continued, the computer becoming a battleground of digital chaos and unyielding defenses. After what felt like an eternity, Jamal's fingers rested. They had blocked the incursion.

As the tension dissipated, Jean slumped back in her chair, feeling the weariness seep into her bones. A glimmer of triumph flickered in her eyes. "Do you have any idea who was behind that?" she asked.

Jamal's expression slid into a frown. "No, but clearly someone powerful was desperate for access to this network. And we don't know how much information they downloaded before we stopped them. I'll check with IT to see if we need to move you to a new location. For now, we'll need to be a lot more careful about your training and we'll stay off the network until everything gets sorted out."

Jean shivered, realizing she had unknown enemies in the shadows. *I will not succumb to fear. I'll focus on becoming stronger and mastering my abilities. The stakes are too high. Failure is not an option.* When she went to bed later that night, Jean's muscles ached, but her mind buzzed with excitement. She knew this was just the beginning of her journey as a Xeno-Human.

28

Fostering Family

The next morning, Jean heard a few knocks on her door while she was getting dressed. She slipped on a robe and opened the door. Jamal stood at the other end.

"Good morning, beautiful," he said with a crooked grin.

"Good morning. What's up?" Jean asked as she adjusted the robe.

"Well, you were so amazing yesterday that I know you're ready for the next step."

"Oh, what's the next step?"

"I'm going to take you to the Bena's' home today. They are the Xeno family who will teach you some things about your heritage and how to manage the extra skills you have because of your Xeno DNA."

"Are you going to leave me there?"

"If you want, you can spend the day with them and I can pick you up in the evening so you can sleep here."

Jean breathed a sigh of relief. "Yeah, that would be great."

An hour later, Jamal drove Jean to the Bena's home in a nearby gated community. The gated community resembled a fort with an enormous stone wall surrounding it. When they arrived at the Bena's home, Jean gasped. It was unlike anything Jean had ever seen before. The house was rectangular and made of stucco. It had two tall, metallic cylinders on one side and a garage on the other. A long, narrow driveway led up to a beautiful entrance with colorful stained glass.

Jamal rang the doorbell. A young boy who appeared to be about six or seven years old opened the door and greeted him with a hug.

As Jean stepped into the home, the smell of moist soil, grassy vegetation, and sweet flowers enveloped her. The otherworldly decor immediately struck her. Green vines and exotic planets completely covered most walls. The hairs on the back of Jean's neck stood up as she surveyed her surroundings.

Jamal gently placed his arm around Jean's shoulder. "Don't worry. The Bena family is one of the most respected in the galaxy. They'll teach you everything you need to know."

Jean nodded, but her legs became shaky as she followed the young boy farther inside, leading her and Jamal to a cozy dining room with curved organic furniture. The other members of the Bena family sat at a small round table in the center of the room. They fixed their eyes on Jean as she entered.

Jean glanced at everyone with a faint smile. *I'm surprised to see them in their human form. Don't they like to be in their natural form at home? Are they just trying to make me comfortable? They look like normal people. I never would have never guessed they were from another planet.* Mrs. Bena was tall and slender with a silver and black pixie haircut and violet eyes. Mr. Bena was also tall and slender with a bald head that glistened under the soft lights. Their children were two young boys who appeared to be less than ten years old. *It would be interesting to see what this family really looks like in their alien form.*

Mr. Bena stood. His black eyes sparkled as he spoke. "Welcome, Jean. Come, have a seat and make yourself comfortable. Jamal told us some things about you, so I will tell you some things about us. I am a doctor and my wife owns a coffee shop. We came to this planet as children. Our sons were born here. Do you have questions for us?"

Jean shifted in her seat, her stomach twisting into knots. She studied the family as they spoke. Their mannerisms were fluid and graceful, reminding her of ballet dancers. *They seem nice enough, but they're still different. And I'm foreign to them. Do they see me as just another human? Or do they feel a connection to me because I'm part Xeno?* "Um, do you remember anything about where you're from?"

"Bits and pieces. I remember running around and playing with friends. I remember school. It was very different from school on this planet."

Mrs. Bena chuckled. "Ah, yes. My Earth teacher thought I was crazy when she asked a question and I danced the response."

Jean's eyes widened. "What did the other students think? Did they make fun of you?"

"At first they did, but then I taught them a few lessons. Let's just say they became too scared to mess with me."

Mr. Bena glanced at his wife and smiled. "Our lessons involved significant physical activity. Schools believed developing physical strength was as important as learning facts. There was no such thing as sitting in a room listening to a teacher lecture. We also learned about advanced technologies at a young age."

"Wow, I wish I would have had some of those skills and knowledge."

"Jean, they were always within you. It was in your DNA. You just needed to know how to activate them."

Jean scrunched her brows. "How do I activate them?"

"That's what we're here for. If it's okay, I'd like to run some tests on you. It's completely your choice, but I believe it will be beneficial to assess your abilities before we try to strengthen them."

Jean glanced at Jamal and he nodded. "Jean, you don't need to do it, but I agree. It will really help."

"Will it hurt?"

Mr. Bena chuckled. "No, it won't hurt. But if you're uncomfortable, you can stop at any time."

"Okay, I'll..." Jean caught a flash of something out of the corner of her eye. It seemed as if something had sped across the hallway. *What's that? Is it some sort of alien pet?* Jean turned her head toward the hall.

"Mason!" Mrs. Bena hopped up. "I'm sorry, excuse me," she said, rushing to the hallway. "Mason, what did I say about staying in your human form? Get back here!"

Jean was shocked to hear that one kid was running around the hallway in his alien form. She never saw him leave the room.

Mr. Bena slammed the door shut. "I apologize. Kids are just ... well, kids are kids. Shall we begin the assessments?"

Jean's mouth went dry. What would the tests reveal?

"I can stay if you want," Jamal said.

"No, it's okay. You can leave." Jean stiffened in her seat and took a deep breath. *I can do this. Jamal's working to keep me safe and he trusts the Benas. Everything will be fine.*

"Are you sure?"

Jean nodded.

"Okay, I'll pick you up later. Does five o'clock work?"

"Yeah." Jean's pulse quickened. She wasn't sure if it was fear or excitement running through her veins, but she knew the tests would teach her more about herself than she'd ever known.

After Jamal left, Mr. Bena led Jean to a large solarium. Bright sunlight pierced the glass walls. The air smelled like a mix of salt, iodine, and seaweed. An Olympic-sized swimming pool was on the outside of the solarium.

As Mr. Bena walked around the room, powering on various devices for Jean's assessment, her eyes scanned the room. A slim metallic door in the corner slid open. With his back turned, Mr. Bena stood there, pressing buttons on a high-tech console. Hovering over his shoulder, a shimmering bluish screen displayed video footage of the room. In it, the image of an alien appeared.

Jean stifled a horrified gasp as Mr. Bena's skin rippled, almost liquifying. His head stretched and expanded, skull elongating. Dark, blank eyes glared from an elongated face framed by tiny quivering tentacles instead of hair.

Realizing the video showed what was beneath Mr. Bena's human disguise, Jean's heart seized. That thing examined her with polite interest mere moments ago! Her pulse raced. *I should flee this place, these creatures masquerading as people. I don't belong here. Wait, what is wrong with me? A part of me is like them. How can I ever accept myself if I can't accept them? Am I a fraud too?*

The sleek metallic door slid shut again, cutting off her view. Mr. Bena turned, smiling pleasantly in his human form. "Just about ready," he said. He pointed to a large machine with a series of dials and screens in the corner. "This is a thermal test chamber," he explained. "It will allow me to test your body's response to different temperatures."

Jean nodded, her mouth dry with anticipation. She had a sense of excitement and dread in equal measure. What if the test showed no special skills or abilities? What if the test caused pain or injury since she wasn't 100% Xeno? Doctors often say you might feel some discomfort, although the result is nothing less than pain.

Mr. Bena stepped behind the chamber, adjusting the dials. A low hum filled the room. He opened the door and motioned for Jean to step onto a platform inside the machine. "That will measure your body temperature," he said, pointing to a small screen on the platform.

Jean stepped onto the platform, her bare feet tingling as they touched the cool metal. Mr. Bena closed the door, thrusting Jean into blackness. She heard a few clicks and took a deep breath to steady her nerves. The chamber grew warmer, and a flush of heat spread across her skin. After a few seconds, she no longer felt hot.

After a few minutes, Jean heard clicking sounds again. This time, the room grew cooler, and a shiver ran down her spine. A few seconds later, her body temperature stabilized and she no longer felt cold. The chamber's door swung open.

"Very interesting," Mr. Bena said, scribbling notes onto a clipboard. "Despite your human genes, your body responded the same way a Xeno's body would respond. There was no difference."

"What does that mean?"

"I don't know, but we may be more alike than I realized. Come, follow me. Next, I will test your sight and hearing." Mr. Bena led Jean to a small, soundproof booth, placed a set of headphones on her ears, and handed her a notepad. "Raise your hand every time you hear a sound and write what you hear."

Next, Mr. Bena led Jean to a small room for an eye exam. She stepped into the small room, feeling like she was in a doctor's office. Mr. Bena motioned for her to sit in front of a large illuminated chart on the wall. He examined her eyes and instructed her to read letters on the eye chart.

"Well Jean, you did great with the hearing and eye exams. You could hear certain sounds that only Xeno people can hear and your eyesight is excellent. Are you hungry? This might be a good time for a lunch break."

"Yeah, that sounds good."

Mr. Bena and Jean headed to the kitchen, where Mrs. Bena was making lunch for the kids. Mrs. Bena glanced at them and smiled. "How's the testing going?"

"Great, but Jean and I are ready for a lunch break before we finish the tests."

Mrs. Bena nodded and gestured for them to sit down at the kitchen table. "I made some sandwiches and soup," she said, placing small plates and bowls in front of them. "Jean, would you like to try a dessert from my home planet?"

"Yes, that would be great. Thank you."

Mrs. Bena pulled a tray out of the refrigerator and set it on the table in front of Jean. There were square desserts that looked like marshmallows covered with green coconut. "They're from an old family recipe. Some things had to be modified because Earth doesn't have every ingredient that exists on Tlatzin. However, we were able to bring some of our plants and cultivate them here on earth. These desserts are made from a type of sugar and vegetation that originated from Tlatzin."

Jean grabbed a dessert off the tray. As she took a bite, a burst of sweetness exploded in her mouth. It was unlike anything she had ever eaten. The texture was denser than marshmallows and the part that looked like green coconut tasted like a mixture of mango and banana. She savored the taste, feeling a sense of wonder at the thought that this dessert had come from another planet. "This is delicious," she said, taking another bite.

Mrs. Bena chuckled. "I'm glad you like it. You can take some home."

"Thank you." Jean smiled. "I may have to take you up on that offer."

"The next test will see if you have the ability to change shape."

Jean's eyes widened. "As in shape-shifting?"

"Yes," Mr. Bena confirmed. "It's a common ability among Xeno people. Based on your previous test results, it's definitely a possibility for you."

Jean's heart fluttered with excitement as Mr. Bena led her to a room with a large mirror covering one wall. "Look at your reflection in the mirror and try to imagine yourself appearing different. Concentrate on changing your facial features."

Jean stared at herself in the mirror. She took a deep breath and closed her eyes. Next, she pictured herself with different eyes, nose, and mouth. A few minutes later, she opened her eyes, but nothing had changed. "I don't think I can do it."

"I think you can. Try again. This time, keep your eyes open. It will help with control."

Jean stared in the mirror, focusing on her eyes. A couple of minutes later, her eyes changed from brown to a light-yellow color. "My eyes changed!"

Mr. Bena shrieked. "Good job! Now, try again. This time try to focus on your entire body. Think about your feet. Start there and work your way up."

Jean stared at herself in the mirror and looked down at her feet. She closed her eyes before remembering the instruction to keep them open. After staring at her feet, she shifted her gaze to her legs. Suddenly, her legs softened and changed into wavy tentacles, causing Jean to plummet to the floor. She kept falling back to the floor as she attempted to stand. A few seconds later, her legs returned and she could stand up. She was breathless and fatigued, as if she had just crossed the finish line of a marathon. "I don't know what happened. I was focusing on my face."

"Don't worry. Tomorrow, we will focus on how to control your abilities. Today, I just wanted to see what you could do, and you did great."

Jean nodded, feeling both exhilarated and exhausted from her moment of transformation. She couldn't wait to explore her abilities further, to see what other forms she could take and what other powers she might possess. But for now, she needed a break.

"Can I rest for a bit?" she asked, feeling a little lightheaded.

"Of course," Mr. Bena said. "Take all the time you need. As you practice changing your shape, you will become stronger. Eventually, you won't lose energy during your transformations."

"Good to know." Jean collapsed onto a nearby couch, closing her eyes and taking deep breaths as she tried to regain her strength. She felt a wave of gratitude toward the Benas, who had taken her in and given her a chance to discover who she truly was. It was a kindness she would never forget.

29

Inter-Galactic Treats

Jamal returned to the Bena's home to pick up Jean. As Jean walked to Jamal's car, the late afternoon sun cast a warm glow on his handsome features. She couldn't help but notice how his eyes seemed to sparkle.

Jamal paused when they reached the car. "How did your tests go?"

"I believe they went well. Mr. Bena said I had skills like people who are 100% Xeno."

"Cool. Hey, there's a neat little restaurant here owned by a Xeno and a human. The cool thing about it is that it features food from both planets. Would you like to go there for dinner?"

"Sure."

Jamal's face lit up. "So, it's a date?"

"A date? You're asking me out on a date?" Jean said, giggling. *Sure Jamal is handsome—wickedly handsome actually. But I can't think about that now.*

Jamal chuckled. "Perhaps. If you want it to be a date," he said as he winked and opened the car door for Jean.

"I'm fine with it either way, as long as you're paying."

"Ouch." Jamal winced, and his face contorted with mixed emotions. He gestured toward a house a few doors down from the Bena's home, a quaint little place with a white picket fence. "See that house? A human family moved there after adopting a Xeno child."

As he spoke, a light breeze rustled the leaves of the nearby trees, carrying with it the distant chirping of birds. The sun cast a warm glow, illuminating the scene with a golden hue. The scent of blooming flowers permeated the air, adding a touch of serenity.

"What happened to the child's biological parents?"

Jamal's eyes clouded with sorrow, mirroring the heaviness in his voice. "No one knows. It's a haunting mystery. The child's parents left him in the care of a babysitter, but they never returned. Abandoned, like a wilting flower left to wither."

Oh, he's a poet now? "That's so sad. I definitely understand what that feels like," Jean said, the words hanging heavy, like a veil of melancholy. "I can't help but wonder ... did Smyte and his people have something to do with it?"

Jamal shrugged. "It's possible. We haven't given up hope they'll be found one day. I was hoping they were at the Genesis Sector, but there were no signs of them there."

Jamal pulled into the parking lot of the Galacade Diner. On the outside, the restaurant looked the same as many American diners. It was small, brightly lit, and had an old-fashioned jukebox on the inside near the entrance.

As Jamal held open the restaurant door, ushering her inside with a hand hovering gently along her back, warmth bloomed through Jean. Her cheeks flushed. Could this dinner lead to something more? *No, he's probably the type of guy who flirts with all the ladies. Yeah, that's what he is. Nothing but a flirt. I bet he has a dozen women scattered around the country.* Her pulse quickened as she took in the cozy, stylish atmosphere around them. As they waited to be seated, the smell of exotic spices danced in the air. A cheerful hostess led Jean and Jamal to a small booth near the kitchen and handed them their menus.

As Jean slid into the booth, her eyes darted around the restaurant nervously. Despite the familiar diner decor, everything was foreign to her. She had never been to an alien-human establishment before.

"Don't worry, we're safe here. We're still in the gated community, no outsiders allowed, but…"

"But what?"

Jamal sighed. "It's just that tensions are growing among the Xenos over the recent data breach. Many families are on edge, wondering if their identities were compromised. Although we encrypt all data, it's not clear how much the hackers could access."

"So more people might know I'm part Xeno?" *Most people won't be able to tell I'm part Xeno just by looking at me. The network hack changes things,*

"Let's not worry about the unknown just yet."

Jean nodded. She picked up the menu with shaky hands and perused its contents. "Okay, this may seem like a weird question, but is all Xeno food safe for human consumption?"

"I don't know, but everything in this restaurant is safe."

"So, what's good? Do you have a favorite dish?"

Jamal laughed. "Everything. I like everything. The entrée I order the most often is the moon fish marsala. It has a mix of vegetables from other planets."

"Sounds delicious. Maybe I'll try that."

"There are a couple of drinks I think you'll really like. One is called planet fusion. It's a juice drink made with berries from Earth and Tlatzin.

The other one is sunburst. It's a carbonated drink with a mix of citrus and a citrus-like fruit from Tlatzin."

"I love berries, so I think I'll get the planet fusion one."

"It looks like you and I have the same taste in food. That's one common thing."

Jean blushed as she closed the menu. "Well, I haven't tasted it yet. I might hate it."

Jamal chuckled. "True, but I don't think you will."

A smile tugged at the corners of Jean's lips. "Mrs. Bena gave me some Tlatzin dessert. I enjoyed it. It was delicious."

"I'm sure you'll enjoy this food just as much."

"Any updates about Smyte?" Jean asked after the server left with their orders.

"Not yet, but an informant inside Smyte's inner circle said he overheard something about Smyte being pulled from the lake. He didn't hear whether they pulled him out alive."

Jean tensed slightly. "Oh," she mumbled.

"Don't worry, we'll find out soon enough." Jamal reached across the table and took Jean's hand. "I won't let anything happen to you."

"Oh, you mean like you kept Smyte from getting his hands on me?"

Jamal raised his arm and made a dramatic motion like he was stabbing his heart. "Ouch, that hurt. You know I didn't intend for that to happen."

Jean giggled. "Yeah, I don't quite know what to think about that. But I suppose everything worked out at the end." Their conversation flowed easily as they waited for their food. When their entrées arrived, Jean couldn't believe how delicious the moon fish marsala was. The spices were unlike anything she ever experienced. "Oh my god, this is amazing," she exclaimed.

Jamal grinned. "See, I told you it was good." They ate their meal in comfortable silence, enjoying the unique flavors and each other's company. Throughout dinner, Jamal frequently checked his phone with a small furrow in his brow.

"Is something wrong?"

Jamal shook his head. "Just monitoring the latest updates. I'm sorry. I don't mean to be rude. We're taking extra precautions—increasing security patrols and keeping a close eye out for any suspicious activity."

After they finished eating, Jamal suggested they go for a walk in a nearby park. As they strolled through the park, the sun began to set, casting a warm, orange glow over the trees. Jamal took Jean's hand and pulled her close to him. She could feel his warmth radiating off of him. His phone buzzed. He slid it out of his pocket, the screen's glow casting his features in an ominous bluish light. "Excuse me, I need to take this." Jamal stepped away, out of Jean's earshot. After a terse back and forth with the caller, he returned, his face marred with worry.

"Jamal, is everything okay?"

"That was Nolan, head of Xeno Affairs. They finished analyzing the data breach and they think it's best to relocate you to an apartment within the Xeno community until we better understand what the attackers accessed. It will be safer than staying with Annie."

30

Advancing Skills

The next day, Jean was more confident as Jamal drove her to the Bena's home. She couldn't wait to learn how to control the skills inherited from her father.

Jamal gave Jean's hand an encouraging squeeze before she stepped out of the car. "After today, you will be one step closer to reaching your full potential. I'm so excited for you."

Jean smiled. "Me too."

Mrs. Bena greeted Jean at the door.

"Good morning, Jean. I'm going to train you today. My husband gave me a written report with your test results. Are you ready to get started?" Mrs. Bena's voice had a melodic, echoing quality.

"Yeah. Mr. Bena said I can do things that Xeno can do."

"That's right. He was quite impressed with your abilities." Mrs. Bena led Jean down the hall as she reviewed the test printout. "We worked with a few others who were part human and you performed significantly better."

Mrs. Bena entered a large room with high ceilings. Mirrors covered one wall, making the space seem even more expansive. Various types of equipment—a rock-climbing wall, gymnastics mats, balance beams, a treadmill, and other fitness gear lined the other walls. Jean even spotted what looked like an ice bath in one corner. The center of the room comprised a large open area with training dummies, targets, and a short obstacle course.

Jean spun in a slow circle, taking everything in. Nerves and excitement dueled within her and she couldn't wait to get started.

"Now Jean, your test results show you have powerful senses and excellent strength, but there is one ability we'll need to work on." Mrs. Bena gestured toward a strange contraption in the far-right corner that resembled a vertical wind tunnel. It was a tall, transparent chamber surrounded by control panels and monitors. "This is an anti-gravity machine that will help train you in gravitational manipulation. With practice, you will be able to use your mental focus to levitate objects and eventually yourself."

Jean's eyes widened. She giggled internally as she imagined herself levitating across campus to class.

"It's an extremely advanced skill," continued Mrs. Bena. "Most struggle to make any progress in the beginning, so don't get discouraged if you can't master it today. Xeno practice the skill during early childhood, and it usually takes them eight to ten years to levitate successfully."

Jean nodded, but she still didn't want to fail at her first big training challenge.

"Now, let's start with some warm-up exercises," said Mrs. Bena. As they began the workout, Jean's mind kept drifting back to the anti-gravity machine. She was nervous, but also thrilled at the thought of being able to float through the air.

After warming up, Mrs. Bena had Jean practice balancing exercises on the balance beam and taught her how to alter her body shape while climbing the rock wall. After climbing the wall, Mrs. Bena had Jean practice moving against gravity in the anti-gravity chamber. Following the practice, they took a break for lunch.

When they finished eating lunch, they returned to the training room. Mrs. Bena showed Jean how to move a small wooden block perched atop a table. She gave Jean tips for focusing on the block and told her how to control each side of her brain to gain control of the block.

Jean attempted to follow Mrs. Bena's instructions multiple times, without success.

"Okay, take a deep breath. As you exhale, think about the right side of your brain. Now, concentrate. Imagine the block moving across the table."

Jean gritted her teeth in frustration as she failed yet again to move the small wooden block. She had been trying to telekinetically levitate it for over an hour with no success. "How do Xeno do this so easily?"

Mrs. Bena tapped her forehead. "Electrical signals control our mental faculties across neural networks and synaptic pathways. But for Xeno, many regions operate at a higher base frequency. When we use telekinesis, highly elevated activity amplifies emissions of electromagnetic and quantum energy waves from the brain." She scribbled a drawing of orbiting electrons and particles on the back of Jean's test printout. "These emanate outward, interacting with electrons orbiting objects on a quantum level. In effect, we manipulate the probability distribution of particles using our minds alone to physically displace matter."

Jean's eyes widened. "So you control objects by altering their molecular behavior?"

"Exactly—down to manipulating atomic vibrations sympathetically with neural oscillations. A supreme feat of bio-quantum entanglement, making mind over matter quite literal for our people." Mrs. Bena smiled gently. "With practice, perhaps you can learn to harness this, too. But don't lose heart at difficulties. You are making significant progress. It may take a while to even make the block wobble. You'll get there. You've done enough for today. Let us try again tomorrow."

Jean nodded, wiping the sweat from her brow. "Can I try one more time?"

"Of course."

Jean took a deep breath and stared into the mirror before her legs gave out and she collapsed onto the floor. Mrs. Bena rushed to her side and placed her hand on Jean's forehead. "Are you okay?"

Jean's body froze. "I-I can't move."

"I will get my husband," Mrs. Bena said, dashing away.

Seconds later, Mrs. Bena returned with Mr. Bena by her side. Mr. Bena kneeled down. He placed Jean's wrist between his fingers, checked her pulse, and pulled out a stethoscope to listen to her heart. After a few minutes, Jean wiggled her arms and legs and sat up, feeling embarrassed and defeated after her collapse.

"She's fine. I think she just overdid herself," Mr. Bena said with a comforting grin as he stood. "Young lady, sit still for a moment. Focus on relaxing your body."

Mrs. Bena crouched down next to Jean, placing a gentle hand on her shoulder. "It's alright, dear. You pushed yourself too hard, too soon. Don't worry. It happens to the best of us. You have incredible potential, but true skill requires practice and perseverance." She reached her long fingers under Jean's chin, tilting it up. "I know you want to unlock your abilities quickly, but growth doesn't happen overnight. And to be honest, your human genes might limit what you can achieve compared to a full-blooded Xeno."

"Our people can mentally manipulate matter on a molecular level. We don't yet know if the required exertion will overwhelm your human brain," Mr. Bena explained.

Jean lowered her eyes as her heart sank. *Kale complained about his alien DNA, but my human DNA seems to be the problem.*

Mrs. Bena gently squeezed Jean's hand. "I only tell you this because it's important to know and understand your vulnerabilities in order to survive. Let's take a break for a few days. When you return, we'll take it slower and focus on strengthening the fundamentals. And more importantly, we'll celebrate each step forward, no matter how small. Okay?"

Jean took a deep breath and nodded with a wisp of a smile. Mrs. Bena's words lifted the dark cloud hovering over her. She was right about not being able to transform in a single day, and Jean looked forward to a few days of rest. She left the training room exhausted, but with renewed optimism.

31

Relaxation Mode

The next morning, Jamal approached Jean while she was eating breakfast. "Would you like to go shopping?"

"Um, I don't have any money." *Actually, I was kind of thinking it would be nice to just relax at home today.*

"Okay, so I'm not offering a shopping spree, but if you need anything like clothes and toiletries, we'll take care of it. Consider it a welcome gift. And it will give you a chance to see a cool mall within the Xeno community."

Well, shopping can be a way to relax, and I can definitely use some new clothes. Jean smiled. "Yeah, that sounds like fun."

As they drove to the mall, Jean gazed out the window, taking in the alien district. It was still so new and fascinating to her. When they arrived at the mall, her eyes widened. The architecture was all sleek chrome and glass, with towering citadel-like spires. Inside, the stores were a riot of colors and aromas catering to various intergalactic tastes.

All mall employees, dressed in their professional attire, bustled about the brightly lit shopping center. Chatter of shoppers and occasional laughter filled the air. The tantalizing aroma of freshly brewed coffee wafted from the nearby café, mingling with the scent of new clothes from the fashion boutiques. The smooth texture of the polished marble floors provided a comfortable surface for the bustling feet of the mall patrons, who, like the employees, appeared entirely human.

Jamal led Jean to a clothing store featuring casual wear designed to appeal to the eclectic tastes of Xeno. She tried on several pairs of pants and a few sweaters and tops. Her favorite outfit was a shimmery blue top made with a slimming alien fabric that shifted with her form and stretchy dark blue jeans. Jean smiled as she rotated in front of a large mirror. "Perfect!" she declared, twirling happily.

"Yep, everything is perfect. Is that the only outfit you want?"

"Yeah, it's my favorite."

After purchasing the clothes, they explored shops featuring trinkets and snacks from Tlatzin. As they browsed the shops, Jean fingered an intricate metallic sculpture. "This place is just so ... foreign," she murmured.

Jamal nodded. "It can be a lot to take in at first. What are you thinking?"

"I guess I'm a little overwhelmed. Don't get me wrong, I'm thrilled to be here. But it's a huge adjustment, you know? I'm seeing things I never could have imagined."

"That's understandable," Jamal said. "I remember feeling the same culture shock when I first came here. It's different from any other place I've traveled."

Jean nodded, exhaling slowly. "I'm really glad we're becoming friends. It helps to talk through all this with someone."

"Anytime!" Jamal gave her shoulder a gentle squeeze. "Now let's go get some of those Tlatzin snacks. I think you'll love them!"

Suddenly, an alarm blared, pounding into Jean's ear drums. A piercing siren split the air, the sudden shriek jolting her entire body. Her heart hammered wildly in her chest as adrenaline flooded her veins. She stood paralyzed, struggling to catch her breath as the alarm blared relentlessly. Hands trembling, palms slick with sweat, she clutched at Jamal's arm, her nails digging into his skin.

Jean's mind raced almost as fast as her heart. Was it a fire? A bomb? An attack? Her whole body tensed as the noise battered her eardrums. She tried to run, but her quaking legs were cemented in place. "What's going on?" she yelled.

Jamal leaned close to Jean as his eyes moved in every direction. "Huh?"

"What's going on?" Jean shouted, her voice quivering.

"Not sure. Follow me." Jamal grabbed Jean's hand, leading her down a portal-like staircase. "There's a bunker below the mall," he yelled. Store employees and patrons crowded the stairs. Fluorescent lights flickered, casting an eerie glow against the colorful walls. Jean moved in a daze, her vision tunneling. The piercing alarm echoed in her bones until she arrived in the dimly lit bunker where the concrete walls muffled the noise. Jean leaned forward with her hands on her knees and shuddered, taking deep breaths to calm her ragged breathing.

Jamal stroked Jean's back. "Don't worry. It's probably just a drill. They do them a few times a year."

"Good to know." Jean straightened her body and leaned against Jamal's chest. He responded by placing his arms around her shoulders. *This feels nice. I could definitely get used to this. Focus, Jean. Focus. There are too many important things to focus on. I can't think about having any type of relationship now. It's not the time or place.*

After what felt like an eternity, a crackling voice resonated through the intercom. "Attention, attention. This was just a test drill. I repeat. This was a test drill. You may leave the bunker," it announced.

Jean let out a deep and relieved breath, her tense shoulders softening. A small smile played on her lips as a sense of calm washed over her. "I think I'm going to spend a few days staying home," Jean said, her voice tinged with a hint of exhaustion.

"Sounds good to me," Jamal said with a wink.

As soon as they returned home from the mall, Jean rushed inside and flung herself onto the plush living room couch. She sank into the soft cushion, the fabric conforming perfectly to the curves of her weary body. Annie had stopped by the apartment to prepare dinner for her. Closing her eyes, she allowed the comforting smells of home to wash over her—the savory stew simmering on the stove, the sweet scent of chocolate chip cookies fresh from the oven. The day's chaos had sapped all her energy and her eyelids continued to grow heavier.

When Jamal entered the room and plopped down onto the couch next to her, Jean peeled her eyes open. "Hey, Jamal, do you ever meditate?"

"Not usually. Well, sometimes I might do a little when I practice yoga. Why?"

"I thought maybe it could help me decompress and relax. I've heard that meditation can be good for the mind and body. I tried a little in the past, but I've never been good at it. I keep thinking about everything," she said, giggling.

Jamal smiled warmly. "Let's try it together." He settled beside her, his leg brushing against her thigh. "Close your eyes," he instructed. "Focus only on your breath, in and out. If thoughts come, let them drift away."

Jean took a deep breath and released it into a slow exhale, the lingering tightness in her chest easing. She shut her eyes, emptied her mind, and allowed herself to simply exist.

Suddenly, there was a knock at the door. Jean opened her eyes and scrunched her brows. "Who's that?"

"Ah, let's see." Jamal hopped up and opened the door.

Mary stood on the other side of the door with a wide smile, holding a large gift basket overflowing with a wide variety of fruit and snacks.

Jean hopped up and ran to the door. "Wow, what are you doing here?"

"Well, I heard about your new apartment and I just had to come check it out and bring you a housewarming gift," Mary said, handing Jean the basket.

"Thanks, it's just temporary." Jean leaned her face into the basket and took a deep inhale, breathing in its sweet fruity aroma.

"Oh, I know. But it's still your own place. How is everything?"

"Good. I'm getting ready to begin my remote classes. Come have a seat," Jean said, setting the basket on the counter.

"Oh, I can't stay. I'm getting ready to pick up Azon from deprogramming and drop him off for his charter flight to Iceland."

"Is he moving there?" "No, we don't know what Gravin and Smyte did to him and how it affected his body, so we're sending him for evaluation at one of our facilities. Don't worry, he won't be there long. You'll get to see him again." Mary gave Jean a warm embrace.

"Oh, what about Kale? Is everything still okay with him and Azon?"

Mary chuckled. "Yeah, they're like new best friends. He might join Azon after getting some things settled with his business. Anyway, I hate to leave so soon, but I need to get Azon to his flight."

"Well, it was great seeing you again. Maybe all of us can get together for a reunion when everything settles."

Mary's eyes lit up. "Oh, I would love that! We'll talk later." After giving Jean a quick hug, she bustled out the door.

After Mary left, Jean slid open the glass door and stepped out onto the narrow balcony. Jamal stepped behind her as she took in the sights and sounds of the Xeno community. Laughter drifted from a nearby Xeno family at a playground. The mundane scene filled her with an unexpected sense of hope. However, as an outsider among humans but not fully embraced by Xenos, loneliness crept in. Where did she truly belong? Sighing, Jean retreated inside to the comfort of her temporary apartment.

32

Reunification

Two months after training with Jamal, Jean returned to college to finish her semester in person. When she entered her dorm room, the aroma of freshly brewed coffee caressed her nostrils, evoking a sense of familiarity and comfort. Emmie sat with her legs propped up on her desk and her eyes glued to her laptop's screen. The room was eerily quiet until Emmie turned toward the door.

"Jean! You're back!" Emmie squealed as she ran up to Jean, flung out her arms, and embraced her in a tight hug. She had dyed her hair blue and trimmed it into a short bob.

Jean smiled as she stepped back to release Emmie's grip. The hug had knocked her breath away. "Yeah, home sweet home," Jean said, dropping her bag onto her desk and looking around the room. It was strange being back at the dorm. Before she left, it had felt like home. Now, Jean had a sense of detachment, as if she were merely a guest in someone else's home. Even Emmie seemed different, but she couldn't figure out why. As her eyes scanned the room, Carmen's empty bed and desk immediately grabbed her attention. "What happened to Carmen's stuff?"

"Oh, she moved a few weeks ago. I quite like having an entire room to myself, but it's great having you back."

"I'm glad to be back. It's kind of weird in here without Carmen. Why did she move?"

Emmie shrugged. "Don't know. I came back from class one day, and she had packed up all of her things and she was nowhere to be found. I checked the student directory and saw that she had moved to another dorm. We had some disputes about Xenos. She seemed to be uncomfortable about the fact you're part alien, so that might be the reason, but I really don't know. But, I'm here."

"Right." Jean threw herself onto her bed, landing with a thud. "Was this bed always this hard?"

Emmie giggled. "Yep, hard as bricks."

Deafening silence filled the room. Jean never remembered Emmie being so quiet before. "So..." *Should I tell her about my parents? What about Jamal? Where do I start? Did someone tell her where I was? Did she know I was safe?*

"Um, I don't know if you know this, but I'm a member of Starlight's student organization."

"Oh," Jean said, breathing a sigh of relief as she sat upright. "I was wondering why you didn't ask where I was. How did you find out about the Starlight Organization?"

"Actually, Carmen and I were trying to figure out what happened to you and someone from the organization stopped by to see you. We followed her to a meeting spot and applied, thinking we would get a clue about what happened to you."

"Those are some major spy skills."

Emmie giggled. Her chair screeched as she slid it from under her desk and sat down. "Yeah, I was gonna message you on that secure network, but I figured you were super busy. And to be honest, I was busy too. They knew I was your roommate, so they gave me updates."

"I actually saw your name in the system, but I wasn't sure if it was you or someone else with the same name. I meant to ask Jamal, but I forgot," Jean said, tapping her fingers on her thigh.

"Jamal?"

"He's my uh, friend. Well, accompanied me in my search for my bio family and he helped in many other ways."

"Oh, Agent Walker. I heard about him. You lucked out. He's one of the best agents." Emmie hopped up and pulled a cordless stick vacuum out of her closet. "I guess I gotta get used to having a roommate again. At least we're free to discuss Starlight without having to worry about a non-member overhearing us when we're in our room."

"Yeah, that's definitely a positive. Do you know if they're going to assign a roommate?"

"Not sure, but I'm trying to see if one of the organization's members will be interested in being our roommate. I sent a group message. That way, we don't need to worry about a random person being assigned."

"I need to get used to campus again. I was getting used to remote classes. I kind of liked them, but it's great being back in person."

"At least it's the end of the semester. Do you have any plans for the break?"

"Not really. I want to relax. I was thinking about having a small get together at home. Would you be interested in coming?"

"Of course!" Emmie squealed with delight.

"Great. I'll also invite Jamal and a few other friends."

"That sounds like fun, and I can't wait to meet your boyfriend, Jamal," Emmie teased.

Jean rolled her eyes. "Emmie! He's not my boyfriend, just a good friend who helped me out. Before I make plans, let me call my parents to make sure it's okay." She entered her mother's number into the phone.

Mrs. Anderson answered in a singsong voice. "Hello?"

"Hi Mom, would you mind if I invite some friends over during the break?"

"Oooh, that would be wonderful. I'll start planning the menu. Your father will be so excited you're having friends over."

After ending the call, Jean turned toward Emmie. "It's official, the party is on! Maybe I'll see if my bio parents can come too."

"Yeah, I heard you met them. I'm so happy for you. This has been such a monumental year. You started college, learned you're part Xeno, and met your bio parents. Oh, I almost forgot—you also met your half-brother. What's next?"

"That's a good question. They still haven't found Smyte. He might still be alive." *Of course, I hope he isn't still alive. Is that a bad thing to say? To hope that someone had died?*

"He's a powerful man, but he's only human. Do you really believe he's still alive?"

"I believe it's possible, and so does Jamal. Even if he's not, there are others who will carry on his work."

Emmie sighed. "Well, based on what I know, he's certainly no match for you."

"I don't know about that. He has an entire army."

Emmie grinned. "So do you. Hey, I was going to head to the cafeteria. Do you want to come?"

"No, I'm not hungry. Thanks anyway."

After Emmie left, Jean sat on her bed and leaned against the wall. As excited as she was to be back, everything felt different. She gazed around the room that had been her home for two months before everything changed. Part of her missed the normalcy of her past college life—staying up late, goofing off with Emmie and Carmen, eating pizza in the cafeteria, cramming for exams. She couldn't just slip back into that carefree routine now. Too much had happened.

She flexed her hands, feeling the subtle power flowing through her veins. Her DNA and the abilities she possessed made her stand apart from everyone else on campus. While her classmates worried about grades and social lives, she now faced dangers they could never fathom.

After pondering her new life, Jean unpacked her suitcase and tidied up the room. As she cleaned around Carmen's old bed, something wedged between the mattress and bed frame caught her eye. Jean reached down and pulled out something that was hard and plastic. It was Carmen's old cellphone. Curious, Jean pressed the power button. Although her conscience nagged at her, Jean couldn't help poking around its contents to see if there were any clues about why Carmen left. Her eyes widened as she read the last emails saved on the phone. One email read, "Here are the photos we discussed. She caught me before I could get more information. Let me know if you need anything else."

Jean's hands shook as she looked at the photos. They were screenshots of information from Emmie's Starlight tablet, photos of Emmie, and a copy of Jean's missing person flyer. She took a deep breath. Why was Carmen sending private organization information to someone? Something wasn't right. Footsteps sounded outside and the door lock clicked. Jean slipped the phone into her pocket and sat at her desk as Emmie entered the room. Her facial expression was blank as she pondered what she should do.

"What's wrong? You look worried."

"Um…" Jean drew in a sharp breath. She was unsure if she should tell Emmie about the email. Finally, she decided she needed to trust her friend. "I found something strange in Carmen's bed," she said, pulling the phone out of her pocket and handing it to Emmie.

Emmie's mouth hung open and her eyes widened as she read it. "This is … bad. Really, really bad."

Jean sighed. "I know. It looks like she sent a lot of confidential information."

"We need to tell the Starlight Organization. They need to know that information may have gotten into the wrong hands."

Jean nodded. "I agree, but we need to be careful, too. Whoever Carmen sent those photos to might be watching us. And I don't want you to get in trouble for what Carmen did."

"Right. We need to be discreet."

"I'll contact Jamal and let him know what happened. It might be harmless, but it's better to be safe. Maybe he can have the organization investigate things without releasing your name."

"Great. I like your idea."

Jean felt a surge of anger toward Carmen. How could she be so careless? Handing over confidential information can lead to dangerous consequences, regardless of intent. Her fingers trembled as they pressed on the keyboard. With each keystroke, she felt the weight of the situation, her heart racing with anticipation.

A few minutes after Jean pressed send, a message from Jamal popped up. *Don't worry. I removed Emmie's name and forwarded a copy of your message to our top people. I also scheduled an emergency meeting to discuss potential risks and solutions.*

Jean nervously paced back and forth, her eyes darting around the walls adorned with photographs and celebrity posters. The faint scent of dust filled the air, mingling with her anxious anticipation. Finally, after what felt like an eternity, her phone pierced the stillness with its shrill ringtone. With sweaty hands, she answered. "Hey, did you find out anything?"

Jamal chuckled. "No, hello, how are you?"

Jean gasped. "Huh?"

"Sorry, just a little humor. Anyway, we hacked Carmen's computer and discovered information about a meeting point. It was a fraternity house near campus. We apprehended the man named in her email and secured the data he received from her. It doesn't appear that he did anything with the data yet."

"Thank goodness," Jean exclaimed. "Were you able to determine if he works for Genesis or what he planned to do with the information?"

"He's not talking yet, but we'll get answers. The most important thing is that we contained the leak."

Jean relaxed her body as relief washed over her. "I can't believe Carmen betrayed us like that. What will happen to her?"

"Apparently, she left campus before we could apprehend her," Jamal said. "We'll continue searching for her. But the good news is that you helped stop confidential Xeno information from falling into the wrong hands. You protected countless Xeno lives today, Jean. I'm so proud of you."

Jean grinned. She had feared turmoil would result from Carmen's actions. But thanks to Jamal and his associates, justice had been served.

"Get some rest," Jamal urged gently. "We'll talk more tomorrow. I love you."

Jean grinned. "What?"

"Have a good night, sweetie."

"You too," Jean said as she sank down on her bed. Despite everything, the Xenos and their allies emerged stronger. With each passing day, she was becoming more confident in her ability to tackle whatever challenges might arise in the future. Her journey was only just beginning, and she looked forward to learning more about her ancestry and her newly discovered family.

THE END

Coming Next

The next book in the Uncovered Gene series is Jean's reunion. Jean will meet more of her biological family members and gain more information about Agent Smyte and her former roommate, Carmen. There is no publication date yet, but subscribe to my newsletter for updates.

Click here to sign up for my newsletter:
https://authorkredd.substack.com/

Also by K. Redd

The bond between brothers can never be broken – but the bond between twins is eternal. For almost every day of their lives, Ryan and Brian Wright have been inseparable. As identical twins, the brothers have gone through everything together. Sharing experiences and milestones along the way, and on more than one occasion, using their identical looks to their advantage.

From breezing through exams to accompanying their dream girl to prom, for Ryan and Brian, sharing each other's lives has become the norm – and little has changed now that they are married men with families of their own. Even now, the temptation to switch places to escape reality is too good for either brother to resist.

But when a case of mistaken identity leads one of them to disappear after being shot, it is up to the one left behind to take his place and search for answers. Now, the pressure is on to find his missing twin – but how long can the imposter keep up the ruse before his family discovers the truth?

Double Play is an intense tale of deception, danger, and the bond of brotherhood. Can one man ever convince the world he is really his twin? Perhaps the question isn't whether or not he can – but rather, whether or not he should.

Acknowledgments

I would like to thank my parents and other family members and friends for their encouragement and support. I would also like to thank the beta readers and editors who gave excellent feedback that improved *Jean's Discovery* immensely. Finally, I would like to thank readers for taking the time to read my stories. I hope they entertained you and I look forward to writing more in the future.

About the Author

K. Redd spends her daytime hours practicing law. When she's not working, she spends her free time writing, taking dance lessons and researching her family tree using both historical resources and DNA analysis.

BB bookbub.com/authors/k-redd

f facebook.com/authorkreddbooks

g goodreads.com/author/show/22355280.K_Redd

instagram.com/authorkredd

tiktok.com/@authorkredd

9 798986 144948